Fears, Fantasies & Freedom

Kate! Continue finding your Freedom!

Fears, Fantasies & Freedom

Krylios

Fears, Fantasies & Freedom

Copyright © 2022 by Krylios

ISBN: 979-8-8315-9848-3

First paperback: December 2022

Printed in the United States of America

Cover Design by Olivia Miles

Illustration by Earl Melvin

This is a work of fiction. Names, characters, places and incidents either are the product of the author's imagination or are used fictitiously, and any resemblance to actual persons, living or dead, businesses, companies, events, or locales is entirely coincidental.

Table of Contents

Prologue: The Fairy 7

1. Ave Maria ……………………….... 9

2. Plotting in the Pines………………... 26

3. Snow and Magma ……………… 63

4. Keep Your Head Up …………… 72

5. Leave the Door Open ……………… 94

6. The Caribbean Tree ……………..152

7. That Used to Be His Beach ………….156

8. Power and Purity ………………..162

9. Coming Out on the Other Side ……….187

Acknowledgements ………………… 233

Fears, Fantasies & Freedom

PROLOGUE

The Fairy
(Inspired by 'Girl' - Jamaica Kincaid)

Make sure you rake the yard and water the plants. Sweep the leaves in the back, the leaves in the front and don't forget to remove the heaps. Don't spend the whole day watching TV and don't spend most of the day in bed; only fairies lay in bed all day. Is it true you only hang with girls at school? Kick a ball. Make some guy friends and play a sport – any sport. Kick a goddamned ball.

Why are you always following your mother around? Stop trailing behind your mother so much. Is one of the girls you hang out with at school your little girlfriend?
One of them better be. Mow the lawn, clean your room and wash the bathroom after school. *But I have school the next day.* Don't you have school the next day when you're watching The Real Housewives all night? As a matter of fact, stop watching the Real Housewives – unless you do actually want to become a fairy.

Fears, Fantasies & Freedom

And please, kick a goddamned ball. Speaking of which, stop playing that Lady Gaga shit, that Beyonce shit, that Rihanna shit; that's all bitch shit, find some real shit ... or go kick a goddamned ball.

Develop a firm handshake, don't hold your hand like that, don't walk like that and definitely do not cry, especially in public. *But what if I'm actually sad or upset?* So, you really plan on becoming that type of guy, I see.

...

(What's so wrong with being a fairy?)

1

Ave Maria

Hail Mary, full of grace;
The Lord is with thee.

"I'm glad we have front row seats to this," Lisa quipped, leaning against the bell tower with a satisfied smile on her face.

Maria could not believe her friend was so enthralled by the ongoing proceedings. Lisa was practically salivating and Maria was disgusted. To Maria, it seemed as if it was the literal End of Days. She watched as fire and brimstone (really plastic bottles and soda cans) rained down from the balconies around the quadrangle.

The quad was the biggest outdoor meeting space at St. Bernard's School for Girls and was surrounded by four buildings of varying heights and purposes. Two of the buildings solely contained classrooms, another one housed most of the 16 and 17-year-old girls and the building closest to the entrance of the campus held the various administrative offices of the diocese.

Fears, Fantasies & Freedom

There was a huge bell tower on top of a platform next to the diocese office building where girls sometimes sat to have lunch or gossip.

"It's not a show Lisa," said Maria looking away, "None of this is right." She brushed down her pleated uniform skirt and crouched to sit on the raised platform where her friends Lisa and Zora stood leaning against the centuries-old bell tower. With a sigh, she let her chin fall into her hand as she looked at the wild scene taking place in the quad. It was nothing like she had ever seen before, but had heard of from older cousins. She reckoned that most if not at all of St. Bernard's girls were either somewhere in the quadrangle or along the corridors and balconies that lined the buildings surrounding it. Nobody wanted to miss this.

"It's a show to me!" laughed Lisa, "We've never actually seen it happen, and now it is. Serves her right too."

"Wow, Lisa," Zora finally spoke up. She flashed Lisa a look that could freeze the Caribbean Sea.

Fears, Fantasies & Freedom

Maria watched as her best friend flipped her long hair and came to sit beside her. Maria noticed that Zora had applied just a smidge of eyeliner today; which of course was banned at St. Bernard's but she knew Zora couldn't care less. Maria wouldn't say it out loud, but she was fond of Zora's rebelliousness.

Zora crossed her legs as she sat and Maria noticed that she had worn *the* short skirt today. The blue and yellow plaid pleated skirt stopped right above her knee even though St. Bernard's only permits uniform skirts just below the knee. Zora moved to take a seat. Her smooth dark skin seemed more pronounced as her arm pressed against Maria's caramel-colored skin when she leaned against her as she sat down. Maria felt something jump within her as Zora leaned against her.

"I'm not sure why you two don't find this more enjoyable," Lisa said looking at the girls with a puzzled look.

"Because…" Maria started, before she was cut off by an empty soda can hitting her leg. "See, what I'm talking about Lisa?" Maria picked up the soda can and held it up to Lisa's face. "How can you think any of this is okay or deserved?"

"Because she got caught being nasty and nasty people get what's coming to them," replied Lisa with a sneer.

Zora ducked a plastic bottle flying toward her as she leaned over and whispered in Maria's ear, "Let's get out of here."

It was pandemonium. Poor Khari Messing was being attacked and bullied out of the school by her own peers. This had been going on for almost an hour at this point. They reveled in sharpening their knives to take out the new public enemy - the new outcast. First they chased her to the nurse's office, then her parents came to get her and even then, the girls were relentless. Now they pummeled the Messings' car with any scrap they could find. On the balconies, the girls were laughing, cheering and jeering as they launched any missile they could at Khari and her parents. Maria wondered if any of the Sisters would come out to stop it, but she had yet to see one. The noise in the quadrangle had reached a cacophony and Maria had really had enough of it now.

"What did you say to her?" Lisa questioned, finally sitting next to her friends on the platform.

"We're gonna go. This is a disgrace," replied Maria.

"It's a disgrace to see retribution?"

"It's a disgrace to see how *good* Catholic girls are behaving. I actually want to throw up," Maria replied, standing up and brushing her skirt off. She looked out into the quad as Khari Messing's mother piled her daughter's belongings in the trunk of the car, ducking bottles and cans as she did.

"It's a disgrace that none of the Sisters have come out here to stop it." Maria said, the sound of her voice heightening. She watched as Khari Messing sat in the back seat of her parents' car crouching and crying. Khari's dad was coming down the stairs of her dormitory with his daughter's luggage in hand. He shouted at the students to stop throwing things, but it seemed the more he pleaded, the more ammunition the Catholic girls got. He finally joined his wife at the trunk of the car and stuffed the luggage in amid a rain of plastic and aluminum bombs. Both parents then hurriedly ran to the front of the car and jumped in.

"And it's a sordid disgrace that young women in Christ have resorted to such violence!" Maria shouted at Lisa, "and that you. You! Are reveling in enjoyment!"

"Khari's a dirty freak Maria, or have you forgotten?" Lisa spat.

"And Christ said we are supposed to love everybody Lisa. Unlike you, I'm actually a Christian that reads my scriptures," snapped Maria.

"Well, if you had been reading yours enough, you'd know that it says people like *them* should be stoned."

"Enough!" cried Zora standing up, as the Messings' car sped past them and out through the gates. "I don't read the Bible and I don't care to, either. I only come to this school because my parents think it will *reform* me. Whatever that means. I don't share any of your beliefs, honestly. But Lisa, you're out of line."

"So, you're sticking up for Maria?"

"I'm sticking up for decency, Lisa." She grabbed Maria's arm and they both started walking. "Let's get out of here."

Both girls walked toward their dormitory as Lisa called after them, "Really guys? Come on. Seriously?"

Blessed art thou
Among women.

Fears, Fantasies & Freedom

"Jehovah Jireh, my Provider. His grace is sufficient for me!"

"Alright girls, stop," Sister Claire called, "The 'me' is flat, I need you all to get it. The concert is tomorrow. Come again, one, two, three!"

"Jehovah Jireh, my Provider. His grace is sufficient for me!" the St. Bernard's choir sang.

"Alright it's not the best," Sister Claire said, squinting her eyes a little, "But a couple of you have gotten it. Good job Maria and the soprano line."

Maria smiled, self-satisfied. She had been a part of the St. Bernard's choir for three years now and at 17 she was practically a veteran. She had to finish her last year on top to make sure that she got into her dream college. As the lead of the soprano line, she knew that that would look great on paper; especially because she was also a part of the planning committee for the annual St. Bernard's Gospel and Hymn Concert.

"Alright girls we'll go through the song one last time and that will be it for today. Five, six, seven, eight!"

Fears, Fantasies & Freedom

Maria opened her mouth and belted out *Jehovah Jireh*. The sound was glorious to her; the voices of the girls in the choir blended beautifully. Her soprano line was doing amazingly and they hit every note. The alto and tenor line were also on par and Sister Claire seemed pleased as she waved her hands expertly directing them. As Maria sang, she knew the modulation of the song was coming up and she readied for it; she would not go flat. She smiled as she hit the note perfectly as did the rest of the choir. The orange glow of the setting sun shining through the stained-glass windows created the perfect ambience for such glorious singing. Maria looked to the front of the chapel at the stained-glass window above the door depicting Mary Magdalene washing the feet of Jesus with her hair. She could feel Mary's gratitude as she came to the final stretch of the song. The harmony filled her ears and the melody filled her spirit, it was like a rush. As she proceeded to hit the final note, the front door opened and Zora walked in, flashing her a smile and silently shuffling herself onto a bench at the back. And there it was, that was the climax. As the song ended, Maria was beyond euphoria.

"Brava, that was exceptional, girls!" Sister Claire clapped, "that is what I expect tomorrow. Have a restful evening and take it easy because we have a huge day tomorrow."

Maria hastened to come down from the choir podium, ready to go to Zora.

"Now, now Maria," Sister Claire scolded, "you know we pray before we dismiss."

"I'm sorry Sister," Maria apologized, hanging her head and taking a couple steps back to rejoin the choir.

"Our father, who art in heaven..." the girls started.

After the prayer, Maria dashed to meet Zora in the back, "So did you like it?"

"You guys were amazing!" Zora replied, pulling Maria into a hug, "I can't wait to see the entire concert tomorrow."

"Really?" Maria asked.

"Of course," said Zora, pulling away, "I may be a heathen but I can appreciate good singing."

Both girls laughed as they left the chapel, "Come on let's go watch a movie to wind down."

And blessed is the
Fruit of thy womb; Jesus.

Fears, Fantasies & Freedom

Maria, as a prefect, had her own room in the Lady of Perpetual Chastity dormitory. She was in charge of an entire dorm room of twelve 13-year-olds. She had to wake them up every morning, give them lights-out at night, tend to their issues between each other and discipline them, if need be. As she and Zora walked through the front door of the dorm, one girl ran up to her with tears in her eyes, "Somebody took my sheets," she sobbed.

"Wait, what?" Maria asked, perplexed.

"Off my bed," she replied, "Come look." She motioned for Maria to follow her.

"Gimme a sec Taylor," Maria said to the girl. She fished a ring of keys from her pocket and gave them to Zora. "Go into my room and set the movie up, I'll be there in a second."

Zora took the keys and walked toward Maria's room as Maria followed Taylor over to her bed.

"Jesus…" Maria swore when she saw Taylor's bed. All her sheets had been removed as well as her pillows. It was just a bare, plain mattress.

"Who did this?" Maria yelled to the entire dorm. Girls started shuffling around and the room grew noisy.

"I said, who did this?" Maria yelled again. Nobody answered and Maria was over it.

"Okay, well if nobody wants to answer then you have early lights-out and if I hear even a peep from any of you then you will all have detention tomorrow and none of you will be allowed to go to the concert."

At that, the girls shuffled into bed, climbing under their covers, while Taylor stood there sobbing – sheet-less and pillow-less.

"Come with me Taylor," Maria said, motioning for Taylor to follow her to her room.

Maria's room was a modest box in the corner of the dormitory. The only furniture was her twin bed set against the right wall of the room, a tiny oak wardrobe next to a chest of drawers on the left side of the room and a small desk and chair next to her bed. There was a window on the right side of the room where Maria hung some basic cream-colored curtains. A crucifix hung on the wall above the desk and it seemed to glow as the soft light from Maria's desk-lamp washed over it. Zora was lying on her bed with a movie queued up on a laptop, when Maria and Taylor entered the room.

"Is everything okay?" Zora asked.

Fears, Fantasies & Freedom

Maria walked over to the chest of drawers and opened the second drawer. A framed picture of baby Jesus in the manger sat on top of the chest next to her hairbrush. "Not really, someone is playing a prank on Taylor. But I'll find out who it is tomorrow."

She pulled out a set of bed sheets and handed them to Taylor, "Use these for tonight, I'll deal with it tomorrow. Goodnight and don't let them get to you." Taylor weakly nodded and moped out the room, she softly sighed as she closed the door behind her.

Maria got on the bed with Zora when Taylor shut the door. "Poor girl," sighed Zora, sitting up. Their legs brushed against each other as Maria got comfortable. Maria felt a chill.

"Yeah, I've been noticing that for a while now," Maria remarked, pulling the comforter over her and Zora's legs. "I fear the other girls think she's…" She paused. She pursed her lips then sighed. She relaxed her shoulders as she leaned with her back against the wall; her shoulder grazing Zora's. "I fear it will turn into a Khari Messing situation."

Fears, Fantasies & Freedom

Zora let out a knowing sigh and nodded, "Yeah that would be tragic." She reached for Maria's hand and absent-mindedly began to play some 'hand game' that seemed to have no rules. She stroked each finger - inside and outside, caressing each knuckle as she went.

"But the thing is…" Maria began, as Zora started pulling her fingers – cracking her knuckles. Maria seemed conflicted with how to form the next sentence. "She's only thirteen."

"And?" Zora inquired, looking up from Maria's hand within hers.

The question hung in the air, waiting for an answer. Neither girl looked at the other and neither spoke. There was nothing to hear except the sound of each other's breathing. Zora still held Maria's hand in hers, softly tangling and unentangling their fingers. Maria tried to imagine what would happen if she got caught in a situation like Khari Messing had. Would all her friends hate her? Lisa seemed to act like she would. Would they kick her out of the choir? Would she get expelled? What would her parents think? At least she knew she'd still have Zora.

Fears, Fantasies & Freedom

Out of the corner of her eye, she saw Zora's face - that beautiful face - and she also seemed to be deep in contemplation. Maria quickly looked away, glancing at the picture of baby Jesus on the chest of drawers. She sighed, breaking the silence and turned to face Zola.

"How do they know?" Maria replied, "Heck, how does *she* know?"

"Don't you know?' Zora inquired, her voice just above a whisper. She traced Maria's fingernails with her index finger.

"Huh?" Maria asked, her throat suddenly dry.

Zora turned to look at Maria as she dropped her hand. She smiled briefly, then looked away for a second. She placed her hand on Maria's once more and opened her mouth as if to speak. Then suddenly she stopped and turned away.

"What?" Maria asked.

"Nothing," came Zora's quiet reply. She reached across the bed and pulled the laptop close to her. "Let's just watch the movie."

"Zora," Maria began.

"Yeah?"

Maria paused, "Nothing." The air in the room became thick; heavy almost, and Maria felt like she had trouble controlling her breathing and her heart rate seemed to increase. She thought it better to let things be.

"So, what are we watching?"

"This old ass movie," Zora replied, "*The Color Purple*"

"Is it any good?" Maria asked.

"Whoopi Goldberg is in it and Oprah, sooo..." Zora replied.

Maria paused, looking at Zora intently, the small talk seemed insincere, "What are we doing, Zora?"

"What do you mean?"

"You know what I mean."

"We're not doing anything," Zora replied, her hand brushing over Maria's thigh.

Maria could feel heat rising up within her. She tried to get it out of her mind but she couldn't. "I don't..." She licked her lips.

"Don't what?" Zora whispered. Her breath felt like a warm, textured breeze as it tickled the back of the hairs on Maria's neck.

Fears, Fantasies & Freedom

Maria turned away, blushing. She got up, walked over to her desk and turned off the desk-lamp, extinguishing its soft glow and darkening the crucifix which hung above. She went over to the chest of drawers and reached for the main light switch on the wall just a few inches above the picture frame with baby Jesus. With a click, she shut the light off. She turned to go back to the bed, then paused, taking a step back towards the chest of drawers. The picture of baby Jesus sat there staring at her in the darkness. She reached out and turned it face down then slowly made her way back to the bed. She sat beside Zora and allowed the darkness to envelope them.

Holy Mary,
Mother of God,
Pray for us Sinners

That night Maria dreamt she was on an adventure. She was an explorer who had discovered a rare cave. A warm cave; dripping. It was a beautiful cavern with glistening walls and shining gems. The air was moist, but it wasn't a sticky, uncomfortable type of moist. It was pleasant.

Fears, Fantasies & Freedom

The more she explored, the more wonders she experienced. An array of blossoms and flowers coated the floor of the cave, extending far out. As she explored the depth, she happened upon Zora within it. She was smiling. She looked radiant. Then she bent down and plucked a solitary flower from the earth. It seemed to thrive within this moist, dark environment. It was pink with lofty petals and a crimson center. She reached out to take it from Zora. She realized that no one had ever done this before. This was her first, and she was at peace.

Now and at the Hour
Of our death,
Amen.

2

Plotting in the Pines

<u>FRIDAY</u>

The sea mist showered my face as the ferry sped across the bay. A white trail followed the ferry, indicating the path we took since leaving Long Island. I loved standing at the stern of the ferry to watch the land slowly disappear from discernable sight. As the wind and the spray swept over me, I watched Long Island fade from a hunk of a landmass to what could be called a mirage in the desert. For some reason I began to laugh. The more the wind beat my face, the more I laughed. I threw my hands above my head and laughed hysterically. Suddenly I felt two arms close around my waist from behind. A jasmine fragrance joined the wind and rode the current into my nostrils. Lauren.

"What's so funny over here, Mister?" she asked, blonde hair flailing wildly in the wind.

My laugh quieted into a chuckle then simmered into a smile. Without answering, I turned my head to the side and found her lips with mine. She rested her chin on my shoulder after the peck and I could tell she closed her eyes as she sighed. The wind danced gleefully in her hair, which was now obstructing my view of a dwindling Long Island.

I decided my solitary reverie was at its end so I turned in her arms to face her as I leaned my back against the white railing of the ferry. She unclasped her hands from behind my back and instead held onto the railing on which I leaned, jailing me in a prison of her arms, her body and the ferry railing. Her green eyes seemed to have a bit of amber just around her pupils in the bright Great South Bay sunlight. I cupped her freckled face in my dark hand and pulled her head toward mine. Our lips locked once more and I got lost in bliss. The spray, the breeze, the sun and the kiss, this was truly a holiday.

We broke the kiss and she leaned against my chest and wrapped her arms around my waist once more. As her head rested on my chest, I looked past her at the rest of the people on the ferry.

Fears, Fantasies & Freedom

There were maybe 35 people on the top deck of the *South Bay Clipper,* most wearing designer sunglasses and pastel T-shirts. There were only four women on this level of the ferry and one of them happened to be leaning against me. The other three were a part of our holiday crew.

The three girls stood out like parakeets among pelicans. Their hair flew about in every direction and their high voices traveled with the wind as they chatted animatedly. Among the sea of azure benches one of the girls stood up demonstrating something to the guy who sat with them. This girl was Sarah O'Toole and the guy was her boyfriend, Caelin Rinehart. Sarah seemed to be in the middle of an exciting story and the others were doubled over in laughter. Sitting next to Caelin was a girl who looked almost exactly like him, this was Kayla, his twin.

Rounding out the group was Lyla Darden; the new girl to this circle, we had only met her at Columbia last spring after she transferred from Brown. Her parents were extremely wealthy real estate developers and she was introduced to us through Sarah, whose parents had worked with Lyla's in the past.

Fears, Fantasies & Freedom

Lauren unwrapped her arms from around my waist then tipped on her toes to kiss me on the cheek. With that she turned around and bounced back over to where the others were sitting. I considered following her but decided against it. They were my friends too, but I was more interested in enjoying the fleeting beauty within the bay than sitting and listening to some more rich, white stories. I looked to the front of the ferry and I could see that we were approaching our destination: Fire Island Pines. My fascination with the disappearing Long Island turned into a fascination for the emerging Fire Island. I decided to move to the bow of the ferry. My friends sat in seats close to the railing on the left side of the boat, so as I walked past them on my way to the bow, I heard Sarah calling out to me.

"Aji! Are you still dreaming or are you going to come sit with us *dahling*?'

I threw a smile her way and stuck my tongue out, committing to my mission. All my friends including my family called me Aji. The only person who called me by my full name, Mauaji, was my mother, who passed three years earlier. I got to the bow and held onto the railing there. I threw my head back and embraced the sun, sail and spray as we pulled into the marina.

Fears, Fantasies & Freedom

As the ferry docked and we disembarked I noticed a huge banner advertising 'The Pines Party' hanging in the harbor; welcoming us to Fire Island Pines. I had never been to Fire Island before, heck I've never been to any island except Manhattan and Long Island, but I did know it was a huge vacation spot and getaway for Tristate area gays. This also means that under normal circumstances, I would probably have never visited here, but Lauren is great friends with a couple that actually owns a home in the Pines so that's how we ended up out here to spend a week.

I surveyed my surroundings as we walked along the dock. The atmosphere was abuzz with life. Men clad in bright-colored shorts and sunglasses milled about the wooden landing, laughing, joking, walking arm in arm and looking not to have a care in the world. Yachts and speedboats stood like soldiers in the marina, sizing up one another as if they were competing to see whose owner had more money. The community had the feel of being its own unique and isolated world where one left all their problems and worries at the dock on Long Island.

Fears, Fantasies & Freedom

The six of us walked together in pairs behind one another, separated by the small suitcases that we pulled behind us. Lauren and I were in front since she had been here before and thus acted as our lead to the Pines Pantry where her friend Servin was supposed to meet us.

Lauren was the first white girl I had ever dated as well as the first wealthy girl. Her mother was a reality star on Bravo while her father was a magnificently successful restaurateur, with multiple restaurants in Manhattan and Brooklyn. I met her during my first semester at Columbia and we kind of hit it off right away. Now it was almost our final year and we were still together, going strong.

My father didn't have much to say about our relationship when we first started dating. I chalked it up to him being still distraught over my mom's death only some months before. Not only that, but we lost our family home and his bookstore when the building we lived in for about a quarter of a century got sold. Commenting on my relationship was the least of his worries. I really took those tragedies hard and Lauren was there to comfort me through all of it.

The Rinehart twins, Caelin and Kayla, walked a few meters behind us. The brown-haired siblings were extremely alike, not only in appearance but also in behavior. They were the kind of twins who actually finished each other's sentences.

Kayla's hair was pulled back in a ponytail which Caelin kept mischievously pulling on causing Kayla to let out a shriek which caused me to keep turning around. They played around a lot, which I suppose is natural for two people who started life together. Though playful, they were also extremely kind and volunteered or supported many benevolent causes during their time at Columbia. I first met them at a donors' dinner I attended upon being awarded a full scholarship to Columbia, which their mother, a dean at the university, hosted. We kind of bonded over having dead parents as their father Count Rinehart had only died a year earlier, leaving them and their mother with a huge fortune.

Fears, Fantasies & Freedom

Behind them, Lyla sauntered along wearing her sunglasses and earphones as Sarah chatted animatedly with…no, *to* her. Lyla, however, seemed particularly disinterested in Sarah's story and more taken with whatever she was listening to on her phone through her earphones. I wasn't exactly sure what to think of Lyla yet since we hadn't hung out with each other that much. I suppose this week in the Pines was a great opportunity for me to get to know her better.

Sarah, I knew quite well since she had been dating Caelin since sophomore year. Sarah grew up on the Upper East Side for most of her life but insisted on speaking with an 'acquired' British affect. Apparently, she had spent three summers in London during middle school and her 'accent' was a result of that. An intelligent girl; she was at the top of all her classes since starting Columbia. During her time there she had five short stories published in renowned prose collections. Despite this, she seemed to have some insecurity about her weight. She wasn't morbidly obese, mind you, but she just wasn't as thin as the other girls on the Upper East Side. Which frankly, should be less of a problem now that she lived in Williamsburg, Brooklyn.

Her parents used to be massive New York City real estate brokers, but their last big deal was the Roberson listing which they worked on with Lyla's parents about four years prior and since then, business has been kind of slow.

As we approached what seemed like a cross between a surf shop, a corner store and a supermarket Lauren lightly touched my shoulder motioning towards the building, "That's the Pines Pantry," she said, "Servin is probably in there grabbing some groceries to make us a huge dinner tonight." Lauren entered the building while the rest of us lingered outside, leaning on the railings overlooking the marina. The sun was bright and beaming but the sea breeze managed to offer a cool reprieve which balanced out the atmosphere.

"We haven't been to the interior yet but I think I might like it here more than Montauk," said Lyla, removing her earphones and making a small seat out of her suitcase.

Sarah, who was standing next to Lyla, walked over and leaned against Caelin who was resting against the railing. "I reckon it's quite alright," she said, "I just wish I didn't feel self-conscious-"

"About your body?" Lyla interjected, "Oh honey, no one here cares. The men are all gay."

"No Lyla, I was talking about being a straight girl on Gay Island with my boyfriend," Sarah retorted, "That's what I'm self-conscious about." She folded her arms in front of her belly as she said this and Caelin wrapped his arms around her, giving her a little kiss on the neck at the same time.

"That was uncalled for Lyla, body shaming is not okay," said Kayla, who spared one moment to look up from her phone to shoot Lyla a judgmental look.

"I never body shamed anyone Kayla," Lyla scoffed getting up off her suitcase, "Sarah, for your information not all of Fire Island is gay. It's just the Pines and well Cherry Grove is like a lesbian community as well, but my friend Reginald and his wife also have a mansion on the island."

"Well thanks for the geography lesson, Lyla," Sarah said "Really bang on information, innit?" Sarah often punctuated her sentences with *innit*, conveniently dropping the 't' at the end. This, we'd all come to accept, was a feature of her 'accent.'

"Aji, where'd you summer growing up?" Lyla asked, turning to me. At this point, I was also leaning against the railing next to Kayla, waiting patiently for Lauren to return. Lyla stood just in front me, peering at me through her sunglasses, her jet-black hair blowing in the wind; waiting for my answer.

"Where did I summer?" I repeated.

"You know, Sag Harbor, Montauk, maybe the West Coast" she answered matter-of-factly. She slowly rocked back and forth on the balls of her feet as she talked.

"I mean; we went to Florida when I was little." I offered.

"Ooh a second house in Miami," she purred, "that's exquisite."

I turned to look at Kayla to see if she shared my puzzled expression. She did. Confirming this, I turned and looked back at Lyla, "I went to Florida twice, once to Orlando and another time to Fort Lauderdale. We did not own a house there. And we've never owned a summer house."

"Oh bummer," she replied, "Well your mom should probably start hanging out with Lauren's mom. Did you know they just filmed in Bora Bora? I heard they stayed in like the biggest villa on the island."

Fears, Fantasies & Freedom

"Kayla, my mom died from cancer three and a half years ago so there's that." I deadpanned. She shifted uneasily next to me and Lyla stopped rocking back on the balls of her feet.

"Guys, this is Servin!" came a voice from the entrance of the Pines Pantry. It was Lauren emerging from the store holding the hand of a tall middle-aged man with sandy hair; saving us from this awkward moment. The man had on light blue shorts that stopped just above his knees and a navy and white striped tank top with a thatch fedora. He held two shopping bags in his right hand while Lauren held his other hand captive.

"Well, aren't you a black Zac Efron?" said Servin beaming as he walked up to me. He unlinked his hand from Lauren's and reached out to me in greeting. I shook his hand and smiled, "I'm Aji, Lauren's boyfriend and Efron wished he had these abs."

"Ooh and he's got jokes," Servin replied laughing, "Lauren, hang on to this one."

"I'm trying my best," laughed Lauren. "This is Lyla, she's very rich," she said, pointing over to her.

"That is true," Lyla beamed, extending her arm in greeting to Servin, "and you look fab, bitch!"

"Thank you? I guess..." Servin replied, frowning a little, then ending with a half-hearted chuckle.

"I'm Sarah and this is my boyfriend Caelin," Sarah piped up, removing herself from Caelin's grasp and offering Servin an embrace. He returned the gesture and he gave her a half-hug with his free hand. As they broke the hug, Sarah spun around extending her arm toward Kayla, "And this is-"

"Thank you, Sarah," Kayla interjected, "I'm Kayla, Caelin's sister."

"Nice to meet you," Servin replied, "Twins?"

"Precisely." Both siblings answered.

"Alright, enough of the niceties, the house is some ways from here, so let's start walking," Servin proclaimed. As we headed off behind Servin's lead, he leaned over to whisper in Lauren's ear, "You really brought two straight men to Fire Island?"

* * * * *

Fire Island Pines was simply breathtaking. The only way to get around was via boardwalk paths or the dirt paths in more secluded areas. There were no roads and no cars.

Fears, Fantasies & Freedom

It was a perfect getaway from the hustle and the bustle of the city. The boardwalks were lined with shrubbery and the residents' personal gardens.

I saw a few people walking by who pulled little wagons loaded with groceries. A deer hid behind a tree as we passed and instinctively, I wondered how deer made it to the island in the first place. According to Servin, the deer were a terrible nuisance who routinely feasted on the personal gardens that residents would grow.

The houses we passed were sometimes similar to one another but most were quite unique. As we turned off one area of the boardwalk Servin called 'dick dock,' he pointed to a gray and white two story building up ahead facing the beach. This house was where he and his partner Chris lived. Servin took us through a side entrance to his house and we ascended a circular staircase to arrive at the second level where a black man wearing a turquoise T-shirt stood behind a counter in the kitchen busily preparing drinks.

"Everyone, this is Chris, the love of my life," Servin proclaimed, waltzing over to his partner and resting the grocery bags on the counter while planting a quick kiss on Chris' cheek.

"Come on in, guys," Chris waved, "put your suitcases over by the hallway and get relaxed in the living room, I'll be right out with the margaritas."

The group of us followed his instructions and were soon served freshly-made margaritas as we lounged in the living room next to the kitchen. We all introduced ourselves to Chris while Servin removed our suitcases to the lower level.

The upper level of the house had an open plan and therefore there were no walls separating the living room from the kitchen. The interior of the house was modern with neutral colors being the main theme of the décor. The only pops of color that painted the living room were the artwork situated along the walls and above the mantelpiece. Big potted plants decorated the corners of the room while a coffee table in the center offered different magazine choices, ranging from gossip rags, to architectural mags to booklets about Fire Island history.

The living room received excellent lighting from the glass windows and doors facing the beach. The glass doors led out to the front porch which had several chairs and tables with umbrellas.

Fears, Fantasies & Freedom

There were five cream-colored couches in the living room; two big sofas and three loveseats. Lauren and I took seats in one of the three-seaters while the twins and Sarah took the other. Lyla opted to sit on a couch by herself, stretching her legs across the upholstery. Chris sat next to me and Lauren after he served us our drinks.

"So, are we all ready to have some fun? The Pines Party is tomorrow night on the beach," remarked Chris.

"I for one am super excited to go swimming," Lyla piped up.

"Sure thing, the water looks really inviting," Kayla agreed, looking out at the beach through the glass doors that led to the front porch.

I looked out at the beach, sipping my margarita as Lauren's hand rested on my thigh. I wondered how expensive it was to live in a place like this. I wasn't exactly sure what Servin's line of work was but it seemed to bring in the big bucks.

Fears, Fantasies & Freedom

I couldn't imagine what it must be like to live in a house like this because I had only ever lived in my family's apartment in Brooklyn, the dorms at Columbia and that facility where I stayed when I 'went away' for a while. Dad and my younger sister live in the Bronx now since he couldn't afford to get another place in Brooklyn. Developers bought the original building where we lived, with the intention of refurbishing, revamping and rebranding.

My parents did pretty well before Mom got sick. She was a successful family lawyer; and Dad's bookstore, located in the same building where we lived, was one of the few 'mom and pop' bookstores left in Brooklyn, so it was well supported by locals. When the building sold, our family lost both sources of income as Mom had already stopped working by the time the bookstore closed. The settlement my father received did little to quell our financial strain. The developers turned the building into an upscale, trendy condominium and the bookstore became a restaurant. Dad, on the other hand, no matter how hard he tried, struggled to open a bookstore in the Bronx.

Fears, Fantasies & Freedom

"And that's when she sprayed string cheese all over her dress!" Chris exclaimed laughing, breaking my train of thought and bringing me back to reality.

Everyone was bowled over in laughter but I had missed the joke, so I threw my head back and feigned laughter to join in. Servin returned upstairs offering to show everyone their rooms for the week. Lauren, Kayla and Sarah followed him downstairs while Chris brought the rest of us out onto the porch. Caelin took a seat at one of the tables while Lyla, Chris and I went to the porch railing to look out at the beach. Dozens of men walked by in speedos and skimpy swim trunks. The blue of the sky disappeared as gray clouds started to roll in, the wind now carried a slight chill with it. Many of the swimmers were leaving the water and those on the beach were packing up their belongings

"There's a storm a-brewing," Chris said.

"Lyla is the one who brought the storm here," Caelin laughed from behind us.

Lyla ignored him and took a sip of her margarita. "I was really hoping to get my feet wet today," she sighed.

"It's fine," Chris said, turning away from the beach. He began toying with the mechanic that operated the umbrellas at the table closest to us. "You have all week here," he told Lyla, "You'll be in the water so much you'll tire of it."

I turned from the beach as well and moved over to the next closest table, setting down my margarita and closing the attached umbrella. Caelin stood up and did the same to the table where he was sitting. In a minute we closed all the umbrellas attached to the porch tables while Lyla stood leaning against the railing watching the beach. More gray clouds rolled in, darkening the sky.

SATURDAY

The smell of waffles and omelets woke me the next morning. I had a long night. Lauren stirred beside me in bed, throwing her arm over my chest and pulling herself close to me. Her head rested on my shoulder.

Fears, Fantasies & Freedom

I kissed her on the forehead and closed my eyes, breathing in the scent of her hair. I gave her another kiss then pushed myself out of bed. Stretching, I cracked my neck as I ambled toward the bathroom. My arms felt a little sore and so did my back. As I said: rough night.

I flipped on the light in the bathroom and stared at myself in the mirror. I had two little scratches at the base of my neck and another one on my shoulder. Man, she really was wild. I turned on the faucet and splashed some water on my face then proceeded to brush my teeth.

Suddenly, I heard a loud smash and someone yelled "Holy Shit!" I ran out of the bathroom, toothbrush and toothpaste still in my mouth to see Lauren sitting up in bed; hair a mess.

"What was that?" she asked.

I shrugged and turned to leave the bedroom to see what was going on upstairs. Lauren jumped out of bed and followed. We lumbered through the hallway as Caelin and Sarah rushed from their rooms as well. Caelin stopped to check Kayla and Lyla's room but it was empty.

"Any clue on what the bloody hell is going on?" Sarah inquired, pulling her silk robe tight and following us.

Lauren and I shook our heads as the four of us headed up the stairs. As we entered the kitchen, the smoke detector went off, piercing the stillness of the morning. I could smell bacon burning.

Servin was standing at the glass doors leading to the porch staring at a smashed plate of eggs lying at his feet. Departing the porch stairs were what looked like Suffolk County police. Servin turned to face us, his face pallid, eyes wide. He opened his mouth as if to say something, then left it there; agape.

'What's the matter?" Sarah inquired. Servin blinked and closed his mouth. He opened it again to speak, but instead repeated his actions from before. Lauren rushed over to his side, leading him away from the door and over to one of the couches, taking care not to step on any of the broken glass. The rest of us crowded around them, eager to hear what had happened.

Servin looked up at us, "They found a body."

Lauren let out an audible gasp and Caelin's eyes widened in shock. "Found a body?" asked Caelin. Servin nodded.

"Where'd they find it?" Lauren whispered, as if afraid of what might come next.

"On the beach, right at the edge of the water." Servin replied, using his head to motion towards the beach.

"Where's Kayla?" Caelin inquired, looking around. He shifted uneasily then shouted in the direction of the stairs, "KAYLA"

"How'd they die?" Sarah whispered.

"They… they think she drowned." Servin answered.

"KAYLA!" tried Caelin again, then muttered to himself, "she must be in the bathroom."

"But they can't be sure till the autopsy report," Servin continued.

At this, the three of us crowding Servin and Lauren slowly took our seats on the couches. I didn't like the word autopsy. I didn't like any word that reminded me of hospitals or medicine in fact. I had spent a good portion of my life going in and out of medical institutions. My mother was perennially in and out of the hospital, and after she passed, I had my own stint in an institution as well. I rested my head in my hand and looked over at Caelin who seemed to be struggling with something to say. Finally, he asked the question everyone was afraid to ask. "Who was it?"

Fears, Fantasies & Freedom

We all stared at Servin, waiting for the answer.

Our eyes were glued to Servin as he prepared an answer. The air in the room suddenly felt like porridge as the tension thickened. Sarah kept biting her nails and Lauren kept shaking her leg. Caelin looked like he was on the brink of tears. Servin narrowed his eyes and pursed his lips.

He sat up on the couch and turned to Sarah, "It's Lyla."

"Wow, what a storm that was last night!" came a voice from the staircase. It was Kayla, dressed in pink fuzzy slippers, a nightcap and peach, silk pajamas. Caelin got up from the couch and rushed to embrace his sister, sobbing. Sarah to my left, burst out crying -- sliding out of her seat and onto the floor.

"Okay, what the hell is going on?" exclaimed Kayla, balking at the scene.

"It's Lyla," Lauren answered.

"What about her?" Kayla inquired, still trapped in her brother's arms.

"Th-th-they found her body!" Sarah wailed, "In the water! She's dead!"

"Ho-lee shit," Kayla breathed.

"We have to go now!" Sarah said, climbing back onto the couch. "Let's all just go and pack our things and head back to the city." No one moved.

"Well, the cops want us to stay put as they're coming by this afternoon with some questions for us to help with the investigation," Servin said. "Did anybody see anything last night?"

"She was with me in our room last night when we both decided to hit the hay at the same time," Kayla said. "The last I saw of her she was gently snoring with a gold leaf mask on her face."

"Fuck," Sarah swore, "we've got to go, innit?"

"I'm not leaving," Lauren said.

Sarah flew off the couch and into Lauren's face. Their noses were inches from each other.

"Your friend just died and you're really thinking about staying on vacation?" she screamed, her British 'accent' slipping.

"Calm down, Sarah!" I called, standing up.

"Aji, stay out of this," she said.

"Sarah, get out of my face, Aji's right, you need to calm down," Lauren said, getting up off the couch. She was taller than Sarah so she seemed more impressive in their standoff. Caelin let go of his sister and moved between Sarah and Lauren, cradling Sarah in his arms.

"Alright guys, take it easy," he said, leading his girlfriend back to her couch.

"I don't know what the rest want to do, Caelin, they're all acting like right gits but let's pack our shit and go." Sarah said as she sat -- regaining her composure and her 'accent.'

"I'm not leaving, Sarah." Caelin said, looking away from her eyes.

"Pardon?"

"I said I'm not leaving either."

"Lyla is dead, Caelin. What don't you bloody understand about that? Are you thick or something?"

"I know. And I'm broken up about it, she was our friend but there is nothing any of us can do about it right now. Going home won't bring her back."

"Can you really imagine yourself staying here and enjoying your holiday after one of your best mates just died?" Sarah asked, her eyes narrowed into slits.

Fears, Fantasies & Freedom

Kayla walked over to where her brother and Sarah sat and squatted in front of them. She placed her hand on Sarah's thigh and said, "One of *your* best friends."

Before Sarah could react, everyone turned towards the staircase at the sound of footsteps. It was Chris. He looked a bit disheveled and I noticed he had scrapes along his hands and arms.

"What happened to you?" Servin asked.

"With what?" Chris asked.

"Your arms." Servin replied. Chris looked down at his arms then grimaced and said, "I had a hard time battening down the windows in the back and clearing the front of the yard in the storm last night," he said. "But what happened to *you* all?"

Sarah stood up, walking towards Chris, "Lyla's dead and I want to go home."

Chris gasped as Sarah strolled past him heading towards the stairs. Chris joined us in the living room and we all began to discuss what would be the best course of action in light of Lyla's death. We didn't have much information about her death except what little the officers revealed to Servin. Her parents had already been informed and her body was airlifted back to the city.

The police said they noticed bruises around her neck, so they were investigating everything. Lauren and Caelin were adamant that they did not want to leave, especially since the Pines party was that night. Kayla didn't think we should stay the entire week. Soon her twin agreed with her and changed his tune. Servin and Chris assured us that they would totally understand if we left that day because of the tragedy that occurred.

I hadn't said much during the conversation and eventually everyone looked at me to see what I had to offer. I thought for a while before I spoke.

"Let's not do a week," I said.

"Aji, really?" Lauren said.

"Yeah," I replied, "Let's just do the weekend. We can get a lot done during that time, then we can go home to grieve."

They let it sink in for a while and eventually we agreed that we would leave Monday morning on the first ferry back to Long Island. At the end of the discussion, Sarah came bounding up the stairs with her suitcase packed.

"I'm leaving," she said, heading towards the glass doors.

Caelin rushed over to inform her of what we had just discussed. She didn't seem to care, and insisted on leaving.

Fears, Fantasies & Freedom

"You don't want any of the breakfast I made?" Servin offered.

"I'm fine," Sarah replied, "I'll eat on the mainland. See you guys on Monday." With that, she planted a kiss on Caelin's face and headed through the front door. Last we saw of her was her burgundy suitcase trailing behind her.

The rest of the day went by slowly and somberly. While most of the group stayed in the house, I went out for a bit. I had a mission when I decided to come to Fire Island with these people and I was going to stick to it. By the time I returned, evening was beginning to set and I realized that the beach in front of Servin's and Chris' was all set up for the Pines Party. Loads of people from the city were coming in for the event and the beach almost reminded me of Times Square at midday, *almost.*

There were men everywhere: in jockstraps, speedos, wings and wigs. It was a cavalcade of color, camp and carnality. This was the biggest event of the summer and all the gays were out. I smiled in spite of myself and headed up the front stairs to see what the atmosphere inside the house was like. As I entered, I realized that it was far different from what I had left earlier in the day.

"You've been out all day," Servin said, busy behind the kitchen counter making cocktails.

"Yeah, I had a… long walk," I replied, rubbing an aching spot on my neck.

"It's been rough, hasn't it?" he remarked.

Before I could answer, Lauren appeared at the top of the staircase dragging me to get dressed; scolding me on the way down for staying out so long.

It seemed everyone had put the news of Lyla's death at the back of their minds. By the time I got ready, the entire group was already a couple drinks in; 'pre-gamed' for the beach party. I grabbed a glass of rum and coke off the counter in the kitchen and downed it as they hurried me through the door. It was time to party.

Fears, Fantasies & Freedom

It was a perfect night for a beach party; a bright full moon hung in the sky painting the sea water with its dazzling whitewash. The air carried with it a refreshing energy; the regular summer humidity that could be experienced in the city was absent in this seaside atmosphere. The beach looked so different in the night illuminated by dozens of lanterns and white tents dotting the expanse of the sand. House and techno pop music blared through the speakers as men grinded and gyrated on each other, throwing back drinks in glee. I hung on to Lauren all night. I'm sure we stood out in the crowd as one of, if not the only straight couple at this party.

"This is really fun," Lauren shouted in my ear.

"Yeah I know," I shouted back, "I'm glad we decided not to leave."

"You seemed really shook up though, you were gone the whole day and you weren't answering any calls or texts." Lauren said, this time pulling away slightly to look into my eyes.

"I just needed some time," I said looking away, "time for myself."

"You didn't happen to see Sarah get on the boat, did you? You weren't the only one MIA. Caelin's been trying to reach her all day," she said.

I shook my head no and drew her closer to me to continue dancing. I scanned the beach to locate Caelin. After a few seconds, I spotted him in the center of a small crowd dancing for spectators. His sister was among the crowd cheering him on. A few feet away I noticed Chris dancing with some guy who was not Servin.

I surveyed the beach for a glimpse of Servin but assumed he was lost in the sea of men on the beach. I looked back over to Chris and saw that he was leading the boy away, up from the beach. It was none of my business. I turned my head away and continued dancing with Lauren. I examined the crowd to see if I could spot the twins, but to no avail. Lauren reached up and locked her lips with mine and I lost myself in the kiss, the lights and the music.

* * * * *

SUNDAY

The next morning was a roller coaster. Lauren and I were woken up by the twins who informed us that they had been in contact with Lyla's mother that morning.

Fears, Fantasies & Freedom

Apparently, there seemed to be some foul play associated with her death. She didn't die from drowning; but from strangulation. The twins were hysterical and packed their bags, telling us they were leaving on the first ferry to Long Island. Caelin was still concerned because he had not heard from Sarah since yesterday and she had promised to call him when she got home. He said he called her parents but they thought that she was still here on Fire Island with the rest of us. Lauren told them that if they thought they'd feel better leaving then they should. By eleven o'clock the twins were on a ferry back to Long Island, texting us every half hour to keep us informed about their whereabouts.

The madness continued with Servin and Chris who had a screaming match in their bedroom. Apparently Servin found out that Chris had taken some boy up the beach. Chris insisted that nothing happened, but Servin was inconsolable and stormed out of the house. Lauren, who was very concerned, followed him, to make sure he was alright. While this was happening, I sat in the kitchen, peeling an orange. Chris came up the stairs and sat on the kitchen stool next to me.

"Are you okay?" I asked.

Fears, Fantasies & Freedom

"Honestly, no," he replied. He reached for the remote on the counter and turned on the TV hanging on the kitchen wall. The news was on.

"Don't worry," I assured him, reaching across to touch his shoulder, "Servin will get over it, he won't put you out."

"Put me out?" he asked, furrowing his brows. "I own this house."

"I thought this was Servin's house," I said.

"No, Servin moved in with me four years ago."

"Wow, I had no idea."

"I work on Wall Street," he said. "Servin's a struggling artist who doesn't struggle that much anymore because he lives with me."

He punctuated this statement by gesturing towards all the artwork on the walls of the living room. I was surprised, I had assumed Servin was the breadwinner in the relationship.

Fears, Fantasies & Freedom

I glanced at the TV for a quick second. Chris reached for the remote and turned it up. Sarah's face was plastered on the screen. Her body had been found in some shrubbery on the island by a couple from Connecticut. Her head was smashed against some rocks. The news reporter mentioned Lyla's death as well, noting that this was the second 'accident' in only a matter of days. They think she fell. I knew better. Chris gasped as the news reporter spoke.

"Oh shit! I know her parents well," he said, "I worked with them and Lyla's parents on the Roberson deal. Something's not right, first Lyla, now Sarah?"

"Oh, you were a part of that?" I questioned, slicing my orange.

"Yeah, I own that property now and without me, Lauren's dad wouldn't have been able to open that restaurant on the ground floor."

"That's interesting," I declared, "I didn't know you were a part of it. I have a lot of knowledge about that deal. I'd assumed Lauren knew you guys through Servin but I now see that it's through you."

I sliced the orange once again and shoved a piece into my mouth. "Well, I feel really bad for Lyla's and Sarah's parents. What a loss."

"What a loss," Chris repeated.

"Sometimes people lose everything because of the actions of others," I said, slicing another piece of orange.

"What do you mean?" Chris asked, eyeing the knife in my hand.

"I mean, I lost a lot," I revealed, looking up from the orange, "You see my dad was saving up to buy the apartment building that we lived in. He also owned a bookstore on the ground level."

"Your dad owns a bookstore?" Chris replied.

"*Owned*," I corrected, "But, then my mom got sick and all the money he saved went to her health. So, after the building got sold, my dad pleaded with the new owner to make it easier to stay in the building. We had been its longest residents. The new owner wanted to make the building a 'trendy' spot however and hiked up the rent exponentially."

"Oh damn, sorry man, that's really…" Chris began, before I interjected.

"There's a restaurant there now," I said, twirling the knife over in my hand. "A 'trendy' one. When we moved to the Bronx then Mom died and Dad remained unemployed, I suppose I kinda lost it. Afterward I spent some time away *getting better*."

Chris reached across the counter and placed his hand on mine, "That's fucking awful, I didn't know that –"

"I learned a lot while I was away though and I came out with a mission," I added, interrupting him. "The scholarship, the University, the girlfriend, the friend group… this vacation." I looked at him. He stared back at me intently, as if searching for something within my eyes.

"Wait, what're you ta–" he began.

"The building we lived in was the Roberson Complex." I interrupted once again, sliding my hand from under his. He looked confused for a second, then slowly I could see the wheels started turning in his head. His mouth fell agape, eyes wide. A solitary tear struggled to hang on to his left eye lid.

"It… it was you," he whispered, tears finally letting go.

Fears, Fantasies & Freedom

I leaned into him, lips right next to his ear and let out a low sigh. I let the orange fall from my hand and tenderly wiped his tears. I still grasped the knife in my other hand.

"All along," I nodded, "What loss the Dardens and O'Toole's must be feeling right now." I pulled back to look at him. His lips trembled, his jaw slackened and the tears I just wiped had already been replaced.

"Please…" he pleaded.

"I can't imagine what Servin is going to go through after this," I whispered, gripping the knife and staring into Chris' eyes. I raised the knife and continued my mission.

3

Snow and Magma

"If you think it hurts, then you're weak. Honestly," River said, quickly wiping away the runny snot making its way down his top lip. He ran one hand through his wavy blond hair and pulled out a bottle of Flonase from his pocket. He gave it a shake and sprayed a considerable amount into both nostrils.

"I've actually never done this before, you know," Caleb replied, staring intently at the snow-like powder on the coffee table. "Just lay off me, Okay?"

He shuffled uneasily into the brown beat-up leather couch situated in the middle of River's living room. Silver beams of moonlight shone through the tall glass doors leading to the side balcony and Caleb reached out, seemingly trying to play with the light in a futile attempt.

"Dude, we got till midnight till it's $35 to get into Magma and you're not about to let that mess happen, hurry and snort it," said River, breaking Caleb's momentary reverie.

Hesitantly, Caleb leaned down towards the coffee table, with one finger pressed against his left nostril. As he got ready to snort, an image of an egg cracking in a frying pan flashed through his mind; *'This is your brain on drugs.'* The image halted him for a second until a decidedly loud sniffle from River beside him roused him from the lull. *It's now or never,* he thought, and with that he plunged his nose into the powdery line and snorted for all it was worth.

It hit him in waves. At first it was like a feather as the minute particles made their way across his nose hairs, tickling them as they flew by. Next it felt like an ice pick skewering his nostrils as the substance settled into the soft matter of his nasal cavity. And finally, the high hit him like a Mack truck, blasting his senses and sending his head into a tizzy.

"Holy sh-," Caleb exclaimed, and before he could even finish speaking, he erupted in a violent sneeze, completely obliterating the remaining two lines meticulously laid out on the coffee table.

"You idiot!" snarled River, "You wasted my shit! I should've never let you try, weak pussy." In a fit of rage, he lunged after Caleb, clasping his hands around his throat, strangling him. Caleb struggled to pry his attacker's hands off him.

He stared into River's blue, dilated, bloodshot eyes; brimmed with malice. In a moment he noticed how pallid his old friend's face was. He noticed the intricate upward coil River's lip formed, the sweat on his brow even though the air conditioning was blasting, the white residue subtly visible on his nose and the slow drip of snot threatening to fall from his friend's nostril and onto his face – he was feral.

It was also in this split moment that Caleb was acutely aware of each of River's individual fingers steadily tightening against his neck. His neck muscles strained against the pressure as his larynx was progressively crushed. He could feel everything, he felt alive – even as less air entered his lungs. He could feel each individual bead of sweat forming on his forehead as River squeezed the life out of him, he could feel the leather of the couch clinging to every section of exposed skin as he was pushed deeper into the seats. He could also feel the pressure rising inside him as his eyes started to go dark, he felt as the muscles within his right arm activated; giving one last push as his fist connected with the right side of River's face.

"Dammit!" River shouted as he leapt off the couch, clutching his face. Caleb sat up quickly with a deep and heavy gasp. He clutched his chest as he wheezed for dear life, "What is wrong with you man? Are you trying to kill me?"

Fears, Fantasies & Freedom

"I'm sorry man," River sputtered, rubbing his face, "I don't know what got in me. Sorry man, sorry…" He walked away from Caleb, stopping just in front of the glass balcony, still holding his hand to his face. Caleb's punch really smarted; the moonlight glinted off his watch as he rubbed his face.

"You need to get your shit together man. Come on let's go, it's 11:28," said Caleb standing up.

River fished in his pockets for his Flonase and took another spray 'for the sinuses' then headed towards the door with Caleb behind him.

They arrived at Magma Lounge at 11:43 to join a lengthy line spanning the entire block.

"There's no way we're gonna get in before 12," River muttered.

"I think we'll make it."

"Well we better, cause I'm not about to pay $35 to get in. They only do this $12 before 12 once a month and I can't afford to miss it tonight.

The Magma Lounge was one of the trendiest clubs in the Buckhead neighborhood of Atlanta. It had three floors and each floor was divided into two sections with separate music, different dance floors and different bars. It was like going to six clubs for the price of one – and tonight it was like six clubs for a third of the price of one. The large building, which used to be a warehouse, added a sense of flair to its surroundings.

Fears, Fantasies & Freedom

Two large searchlights shone into the sky which could be seen from miles away. The façade of the building featured a neon sign above the door with the word MAGMA superimposed on an animation of a volcano erupting; the lava ran down the sides of the first M and the last A. Three bouncers stood at the door; one checked for IDs, the other did a pat down and the final one collected the entry cover.

"You left that stuff at home, right?" asked Caleb as he and River moved up the queue.

"Of course, I did. I'm not that much of an idiot, Caleb."

"I'm just making sure, cause you know you got a penchant for doing some crazy stuff."

It was 11:57 now and the guy in front of River was getting his ID checked by the bouncer. After making sure the guy was of legal age, the bouncer waved him over to get searched by his colleague. As River stepped toward him, the bouncer checked his watch.

"You just about made it, son. ID."

River pulled out his wallet and presented his ID to the bouncer. After a couple of seconds, the bouncer returned his ID and waved him over to be searched. The second bouncer took a longer time with River as he patted down his torso, his front pockets, his back pockets and even his ankles.

"What's this?" the bouncer asked, motioning to River's right front pocket.

"Oh, it's just my nasal spray," River replied, pulling out his Flonase, "for my sinuses. Allergies y'know?"

"Sure, whatever, go ahead."

Both boys made it into the club, just in time, River moved on and paid the last bouncer and then entered the club with Caleb following close behind him. The first section of the club was heaven – if heaven had dozens of strobe lights, gorgeous women, flowing liquor and a pounding 808 beat.

Club patrons were joyfully gyrating and prancing on raised platforms in response to the music. The floor itself was crammed with bodies and faces and limbs all entangling and disentangling in frenzied mirth and elation. The lights, the sounds and the energy on the dance floor became the life force within Caleb's veins. It was all he wanted – no, needed. Every beat of music vibrated his soul, fireworks erupted from his body with everybody that he touched.

He had never felt so euphoric in all his life. A beautiful girl with long box braids started grinding on him and he was immediately exhilarated. They danced for what felt like an eternity. Her cappuccino skin glistened with sweat as the strobe lights reflected off it. Her crop top revealed a single diamond stud swinging from her navel. She laughed and threw her head back then locked lips with him in a moment of ecstasy and unhinged joy.

Nothing could stop this overwhelming feeling, he needed nothing else in life, he was invincible and there wasn't anything else that mattered.

Caleb felt as if he was going to explode and then suddenly a dejected feeling passed through him. At first, he thought it was momentary, but it grew worse. He pushed the girl off him and walked off the floor. A sudden and deep form of depression washed over him and he couldn't understand how or why. The music no longer did anything for him, he felt hot and sticky and also really tired. He looked around for River; he had to get out of there. In a lethargic daze, he stumbled across the floor, pushing through various bodies looking for his friend. He spotted him on top of one of the platforms violently pushing off some girl. Since the platform was not too high, she only stumbled as her feet met the main floor again.

"Hey man, get down!" Caleb shouted. He ran over to check if the girl River had pushed off the platform was okay; she was trying to regain her footing in her six-inch heels, "I'm sorry about him, he's had too much already."

"I haven't had too much, shut the hell up Caleb," retorted River jumping off the platform. "What's your name, hun?" he asked the girl.

"Miranda." The girl replied, shouting above the pounding bass. She seemed utterly disinterested in any conversation River was trying to pursue.

Fears, Fantasies & Freedom

"My name's River. Yeah, I bet you can't think of another River, can you? Except maybe River Phoenix." He spoke a mile a minute and Miranda kept looking around uneasily, eager to escape the unwanted conversation.

As this exchange took place Caleb noticed a flashing blue and red coming through the windows outside.

"River, let's get out of here," Caleb offered.

River ignored him as he leaned against the wall behind him, "Don't you see me in a conversation? Yeah, as I was saying. Most people do. I'm exotic like that."

"Right," Miranda replied drily, "So I'm assuming you've had a little to drink already, right? Cause you seem more than a little lit up right now."

"I should've brought it in where my cock is, you know they don't check there," said River, leaning into Miranda's ear.

"Huh?" Miranda quipped.

"River come on; we need to go." Caleb pleaded as anxiety gripped him.

"The coke, man," River said, speaking to Miranda and once again ignoring Caleb, "The coke. I should have snuck it in on my cock. They never check there."

"Um…"

Fears, Fantasies & Freedom

"Yo, I'm sorry about him. He's not right. Just ignore him please," Caleb said to Miranda hurriedly, while pulling River away. "We have to go now! And why are you talking about coke with some random stranger? Are you crazy?"

"I'm just pissed I had to pay for it here, when I have my own at home" River replied nonchalantly, flashing a small bag at Caleb.

"Wait, what?"

Abruptly, the music stopped and the lights came on instantly blinding the hundreds of club patrons. About a dozen police officers entered the club with batons raised.

"Nobody, move! This is a raid!"

"Shit," muttered Caleb.

River, with his eyes unfocused as ever, beads of sweat coating his brow and an audible sniffle, reached into his pocket and pulled out his Flonase, "Damn allergies."

4

Keep Your Head Up

"OK, how much longer til' the Uber gets here?" Neil asked, turning to his older cousin. Sighing exasperatedly, he wiped the sweat off his brow with the back of his hand and leaned back on the cream-colored column of the porte cochere. He fanned his hand in front of his face, pleading with the dry Las Vegas air to grant him even a slight reprieve from the perpetual heat.

Darnell, his older cousin, was also desperately fanning his face, but with both hands. "Ugh! I knew I shouldn't have left the fan in the room," he said, reaching into his pocket for his cellphone.
"Yeah, yeah, yeah, you were right. But I mean there's gonna be AC in the car and when we get to the dispensary, it will also have AC. It's not like we're walking there," Neil replied.
Darnell looked up from his phone and shot Neil a condescending look. "*Girl.*"
Neil chuckled, "*Girl,* what? Just tell me when the Uber is getting here cause I'm actually about to melt out in this bitch."
"It says four minutes but I feel like it said that three minutes ago."

Neil rolled his eyes, "Shit."

It was Darnell's idea for them to come to Vegas for a few days to help raise Neil's spirits. Neil jumped at the idea as it had been a rough three and a half months since his boyfriend passed and there was no better place to forget one's problems than Vegas. A slight breeze blew through the porte cochere to Neil's relief. The palm trees lining the streets danced ever so gently and graciously in the breeze as taxis and car services pulled up and pulled out of the porte cochere. The Mandalay Bay resort entrance was hustling and bustling this morning as multiple different families and groups of friends passed them by. For Neil, it was a refreshing change of pace to be around people again and being able to go outside instead of lying around in bed all day and watching hours of mind-numbing TV - something which he had gotten much too accustomed to in the past few months. Since they arrived two days ago, Darnell had kept them busy with excursions, excitement and the exploration of the insurmountable tourist traps that Las Vegas had to offer. They had only two days left on the trip and Neil was already dreading going back home to Virginia to be alone with his thoughts in his empty apartment.

"Alright, that should be him pulling up in the Sorento," said Darnell, tapping Neil on the arm and pointing to an approaching black SUV.

Fears, Fantasies & Freedom

"About time," Neil said excitedly, clapping his hands. He was itching to start today's adventure.

"Darnell?" the Uber driver questioned as he pulled in front of them.

"Yup! That's us," Darnell said, jumping into the back of the vehicle with Neil following close behind him. They pulled out of the resort and took off for the dispensary.

"Hey you know if you take an Uber or Lyft to the dispensary they give you extra weed, right?" said the driver looking at us in the rearview mirror.

"Why d'ya think we're here right now?" laughed Darnell. "The first day we got here, we took a Lyft to the dispensary right after we checked in cause we really wanted to try the good shit y'all have out West and our driver told us the same thing. I was gagged when they gave me an extra gram."

"When did you two get here?" the driver asked.

"Just two days ago," Darnell answered, "It's my cousin's first time in Vegas."

"Oh, a first-timer, eh?" The driver drawled. "Pro tip, first timer: everybody's tryna sell you something and if it don't look like they're tryna sell you something then you just ain't looking hard enough. Always something else 'neath the surface."

"I feel like that's the entire premise of this town," Neil remarked, "Everything's a show. It's all big and bold and boisterous and over the top so you buy into it, it's easy to get lost in it all."

"Ah! Good head on this one," the driver noted, "I've been lost in it since I came here 'bout twelve years ago. It ain't for everybody, but some of us like the show."

Neil stared through the window as Darnell and the driver struck up a conversation. Even in the day, without the obvious flashing lights, the city was still a sight to behold. They drove past a billboard featuring two scantily clad women balancing martinis on trays while sitting on a rocket blasting off. Its caption read: LET'S TAKE YOU OUT OF THIS WORLD. Neil wondered if it was advertising a strip club with a space theme or a virtual reality galaxy themed experience with sexy waitresses. Neither would be out of character for Vegas. Neil leaned into the absurdity of his surroundings. He loved that everything and everywhere had a theme and you could visit kitsch versions of New York, Paris or even Egypt all in one night while walking the street with a beer in your hand. He liked the excess, he liked the performance, he liked the artifice. He liked it all, because it pulled him away from the turmoil he experienced when he was alone with his thoughts. He could either choose to get away and get lost in the flash, folly and farce of Vegas or get lost in the tumult and turbulence of his own mind.

Soon they pulled into the parking lot of the dispensary. There was a short line of customers leading to the door of the building. Their driver pulled up to a section of the lot that noticeably had other Ubers or Lyfts.

"I can just jump out and get what I'm getting and you'll wait, right?" Darnell asked our driver.

"Sure thing, just don't take too long," he replied.

"Neil, you coming?" Darnell inquired, opening the car door.

"Nah, just make sure you get the gummies and a few cookies too. And let's hurry it up, I'm starving. We should get some brunch back at the resort."

"Bitch, you're always hungry," Darnell shot back, getting out of the car. "Alright, I'll be quick."

With that, he shut the door and sashayed over to join the line of people getting their IDs checked at the door. Neil did not feel the desire to go stand with his cousin in the 100°F heat when he could chill in the air conditioning while the car idled.

In addition to being Neil's cousin, Darnell was also his best friend. At 28, he was three years older than Neil and they grew up as close as brothers. They had the same interests, similar hobbies, identical musical tastes and happened to be the only gay ones in the family.

Fears, Fantasies & Freedom

Neil had no idea how he would've survived his late boyfriend's untimely death if Darnell had not been there checking in on him every day. But that's how they'd always been: having each other's backs. For both, it was difficult growing up in a Black, religious family. Nobody else understood them or their experiences like they understood each other. They had each seen the other at their absolute lowest and shared so many adventures at their utmost highest. Nell and Neil. That's what the cousins were collectively called since they were children. There's no one else Neil would have rather been doing this trip with, Darnell always knew how to have a good time. He was outgoing, impulsive and bold; a true extrovert. Neil, to his credit, was also confident and gregarious but not quite as extemporaneous as his spontaneous cousin.

Once when they were teenagers, they went to Washington, D.C. together to tour all the museums of the Smithsonian. While on their jaunt from one location to the next they encounter a group of high school seniors on their own tour of the various museums. Within this group was a tall, curly-haired guy that Neil instantly started crushing on. After glimpsing him in the Natural History Museum and then exchanging smiles in the American Art Museum, Neil told himself (and Darnell) that he would approach the guy if they ran into him again.

Fears, Fantasies & Freedom

  Lo and behold, there they were at the Space Shuttle exhibit in the Air & Space Museum and Curly-haired Guy and his group were just across the room from them. Curly-haired Guy spotted them and shot Neil another smile and a wave this time for good measure. Neil smiled and returned the wave but felt quite bashful to walk over to him. Darnell, ever daring, whispered that he'd soon be back and skipped over to the guy. They had a brief conversation, then Darnell returned showing Neil his phone screen with a number typed out.
  "That's his digits, bitch. He said to text him, they're only in town for a couple more days."
  He decided he would adopt Darnell's YOLO attitude while in Vegas and just live in the moment. Even though he was only halfway through his twenties, Neil was more aware of his own mortality and the impermanence of things than he'd ever been before.
  "Alright, you ready?" Darnell's voice startled Neil, jolting him out of his mired mind. He hadn't realized Darnell had already returned.
  "Huh?" Neil asked, a little disoriented.
  Darnell looked at him knowingly.
  "It's all good. Keep your head up. Look! I've got treats!"
  He held up various vacuum sealed packets of sour gummies, cookies and about seven grams of cannabis. He opened the packet with the weed and held it to his nose, inhaling deeply.

"That's that Blue Dream baby, get into it!" He handed Neil the packet and he took a whiff as well. It smelled divine.

"Oooh yaaas! It's giving!" he squealed.

He started clapping to a beat and singing "It's bout to get lit bitch, it's bout get lit bitch!" Darnell joined in with the song and the cousins sang and danced in the backseat as the car pulled out of the lot, heading back to the resort.

Since Nell and Neil had spent the previous days of their trip trekking up and down the Strip, seeing the sights and sounds and indulging in so much of what it had to offer, they decided that they would use today to actually explore the resort where they were staying.

One thing about Vegas is that once you've seen a few casinos, you've seen them all. Neither of the men were gamblers either, so they were more interested in the attractions, exhibits and varying experiences that each location contained to entertain the vacationers who were not holed up in front of a slot machine.

After brunch, they took some edibles (for dessert, Darnell said) and commenced exploring Mandalay Bay. Looking for a more subdued vibe as they rode the waves of the high; they went to the Shark Reef aquarium located in the hotel.

Fears, Fantasies & Freedom

The cousins leisurely sailed through the different sections of the aquarium in wide-eyed marvel at the magnificent marine species present at the exhibit. Neil got lost in it all. One moment he was in a tropical getaway in wonder of every color, shape, size and pattern of fish than he could fathom; next he was sailing down a jungle river as dragons and monsters slithered and slunk just out of reach; then before he knew it, he was on an oceanic voyage in absolute awe of the imposing teeth, tails and fins of ancient predators staring back at him. Keen on prolonging their aquatic adventure, they ventured next to the virtual reality Undersea Explorer exhibit then topped that off with a lazy lounge in a cabana at the beach club.

"I think I'm going to take one more dip then we can head up to the room," Darnell said, getting up to stretch as he basked in the rays of desert sun. The sunlight glinted off his gold-framed sunglasses as he turned his head from side to side creating two distinct cracking sounds as he released the tension in his neck. His mahogany skin gleamed in the sunshine and he wore tiny magenta swim trunks with a palm tree print; reminiscent of the palm trees surrounding the hotel and scattered along this fake beach.

"I'll come with you, my high is wearing off" Neil declared, standing up and stretching as well. He relished the feeling of the sand between his toes.

Fears, Fantasies & Freedom

When they first arrived at the hotel a few days prior, Neil was puzzled when he saw a sign that said BEACH CLUB. As far as he knew, they were in the middle of the desert, not by the seaside. But of course, they would have a fake beach in Vegas, complete with sand, palm trees and actual waves in the water. Children were building sandcastles while their parents relaxed with a good book and a pina colada on beach lounges, a group of athletic young men were far out in the water horseplaying while a few bikini-clad women sat near the water's edge letting their feet get wet by the waves rolling into the 'shore'. Neil chuckled to himself and shook his head; an entire seaside scene in the shadow of the hotel's towering golden facade. This was the kind of absurdity in this town that he'd come to almost admire. He found its shamelessness - at the very least - a little endearing.

Darnell nudged Neil in the side, "Oh wow, look up!" he said. Flying above them was an airplane with a banner trailing behind it that read: AIM FOR THE STARS, SEE THE UNIVERSE. "Well, that's encouraging, ain't it?" Darnell remarked, playfully tousling his shorter cousin's hair.

"Is it though?" Neil replied, looking up and pointing, "Look."

Another plane followed the first and its message read: JOIN US TONIGHT AT 10. GET UR TIX NOW!

"They're always trying to fucking sell us something, huh?" Darnell laughed, running towards the water. Neil followed behind, taking a deep breath before diving in. They spent the next 20 minutes swimming before retreating to their suite. There, they ordered room service and passed out after their respective meals - napping for a couple hours. They woke as evening approached, ready for another night on the town.

"So, what's the plan for tonight, cuz?" Neil asked, stepping out of the bathroom after a long hot shower. He walked over to the mirror where Darnell was styling his hair and grabbed the bottle of facial moisturizer. He pumped a dab of moisturizer in his palm, then rubbed his palms together before slapping them against his cheeks and massaging the serum into his skin.

"Okay so we're gonna get drinks at Miracle Mile then catch a show at Planet Hollywood."

"I mean, I'm here for the drinks, but Nell, we've seen a show every night since we've been here," Neil complained while applying deodorant to his underarms.

Darnell scoffed. "And bitch have you not been getting your life?"

"Of course, they've all been amazing. I especially lived for the drag show at the Flamingo last night but I just wanted to do something a little different tonight. I think I've had my fill of the stage. Let's get off the Strip and find something else to do."

Darnell rolled his eyes and walked over to his side of the suite, picking up and placing his suitcase on the bed. "You're lucky I got these tickets comped," he muttered, rifling through the suitcase for tonight's outfit. "Cause if I had actually paid for them with my own money, you know I'd drag your ass over there."

"Well, why don't we do something free then?" Neil responded, "Let's take some edibles and go to Fremont Street. I bet zooming zooted on the zipline is an experience like no other."

"Hmm, I'm into that. And we can just hang out there and see where the night takes us," Darnell said. "There's always something to get into. Come on, let's get dressed and I'll order the Uber."

Fremont Street buzzed and swayed as crowds moved swiftly under the river of lights and colors from above. Four young women whizzed by overhead on the zipline, screaming their heads off. There were street performers and street artists up and down the street. Families were taking pictures and college-aged kids were laughing, enjoying their moment in Vegas.

Fears, Fantasies & Freedom

As Nell and Neil walked down the street, Neil noticed a small crowd gathering just up ahead. The men walked over. It was a four-man dancing freestyle group. One of the dancers spotted Neil and came over to dance right in front of him; spinning, twirling and flipping around like it was second nature to him. He ended his performance with a one-hand handstand and Neil applauded him frantically.

"Nice to meet you, I'm Noah" he said, extending his arm for a handshake. Neil took his hand and gave it a firm squeeze, "Neil," he replied, "And that's my cousin Darnell." Darnell said hi and waved.

"That was really impressive, Noah," Neil offered.

"Well, thank you, I've been coming out here for about a year and making a little extra cash on Fremont. Tips?" he asked, holding out his hand. Darnell pulled out a fiver and slapped it in his palm, "More where that came from," he winked.

Noah was shirtless and had a gray hoodie tied around his waist with black joggers and a pair of silver and black Levi's sneakers. He signaled to the other three dancers and they came over. "This is Lemar, Jay and Ky," Noah said, introducing them. They all held out their hands which we shook.

"So, what do boys like yourself get up to around this time of night in these parts? Except for the street dancing. We want to experience some hidden gems."

"Actually, we're headed out to a gathering in the desert in a few minutes," Jay said.

"A gathering?" Nell and Neil repeated.

"Yup, some party north of here that I keep hearing people mention. Seems like the place to be tonight," Ky finished.

"Alright, I'm game," Neil said, getting excited.

"Ok sweet, let's get off Fremont and jump in my ride." Lemar states.

Lemar's ride was a 2018 Lexus ES 350 and Darnell whistled when he saw it, "Nice whip man."

"Thanks, I take care of her real well," Lemar responded.

The four of them got in, with Lemar and Ky up the front and Noah joining Jay, Nell and Neil in the back. The windows were down as they cruised on the freeway towards the desert. The desert night was cool and the wind crisp. Neil shoved his arm through the window, closed his eyes and just settled into the highway cruise.

"So, is there a dress code for this party or do you not know?" asked Darnell.

"Uh, I don't think so man. It's pretty chill like that from what I've heard." Ky replied.

"Anybody want shrooms," Jay asked, holding up a baggie of twisted, long-stalked mushrooms.

"Oh yeah I'll certainly try some," Darnell jumped at the bag.

"I'll try some too," Neil added, "Love me a good desert trip."

"Don't forget about me," Ky shouted from up front. They all said Cheers! as each ate a helping of mushrooms. "Ugh," Neil fake retched, "Still tastes nasty."

They got to the desert within half an hour and spread out over the plain was a massive glow-stick party. The music was blasting and people were dancing. There was a huge sign above the DJ booth that said 'The Utmost for the Highest.' Neil chuckled as he thought about how fitting it was, considering the state he was in.

The gathering was set in a wide desert plain with nothing around except for a few cacti and a pile of rocks over by the canyon. Noah grabbed Neil's waist and proceeded to dance with him. They were a little messy but really fun. A few fellow dance floor junkies got roped into the mix and eventually both Neil and Noah each had a pair of glow stick rings around their necks. Noah danced with a lot of finesse, but Neil was holding his own as a partner. The other guys were just moving to the music and riding out the shroom trip that just seemed to have taken off.

Fears, Fantasies & Freedom

The sign next to the sign above the DJ read ALWAYS KEEP YOUR HEAD UP with two green alien heads seemingly giving the other a mischievous smile.

The mushrooms were really starting to kick in and Neil leaned into the music and swayed to the beat. Neil didn't want to think; he just wanted to float and sway. He didn't want to dwell in the grief or the pain of loss. He was doing exactly what he came to Vegas to do. He wanted to forget and he wanted to feel…or maybe not feel. He paused dancing for a bit and scanned the crowd. Darnell was dancing away with the other guys they met at Fremont. They all seemed to be in a trance. Soon Neil and Nell's eyes met and Darnell mouthed, "Are you okay?" Neil nodded and signaled with his head toward the canyon then grabbed Noah by the hand.

"Be safe", Darnell mouthed.

And with that Neil and Noah went walking toward the vicinity of the canyon. When they got a good distance away from the party, they climbed up a hefty plateau with a cliff overlooking the canyon.

Fears, Fantasies & Freedom

Neil laid his head in Noah's lap as he rode on the waves of the trip. In another time, he would've been here with another person. A person he loved, that was now gone. He opened his eyes and looked deep into the night sky. He could make out the different constellations and both Jupiter and Saturn were risen. Nobody really knows what happens after we die, Neil liked to believe that we returned to the stars. Maybe that's where his late boyfriend was; etched once again into the cosmic tapestry. Due to the shroom trip, the stars appeared to dance together in Neil's vision. A light breeze blew by the boys as Noah rubbed Neil's head. Neil leaned against Noah's hand and before you knew it, they were kissing and caressing like crazy on the cliffside. Lots of touching and grabbing and heavy petting.
The ecstasy by this point was fueled by the euphoria and excitement brought on by the shrooms.

"Damn," Neil said between kisses, "I just knew I had to have your fine ass, after I saw you dancing on Fremont."

Noah chuckled a bit, said thanks then went back to snogging. Neil didn't really think about how soon was too soon since the death of his boyfriend, but right now was the right time to have this trippy make out sesh with Noah.

Fears, Fantasies & Freedom

Out the corner of his eye, Neil spotted a tiny but quickly growing pinprick of light in the sky. He broke their kiss for a minute and stared. Noah looked in the same direction. The light grew larger and larger as they watched.

"What is that?" Noah wondered out loud.

"That's not a star", Neil replied. "But whatever it is, is coming here. And fast"

Neil sat up as the unknown object grew larger and hurtled toward them. As it got closer, Neil could make out that the object was cylindrical in shape and very tall. It got closer and closer till the mammoth cylinder was floating just above their heads. Suddenly, a huge flash of light emerged from the object that slowly bathed Neil and Noah. The light's color was somewhere between cream and sterling silver and both guys were left spellbound seeing such a sight.

Soon two large sections of the cylinder opened up and more light flowed out. Neil couldn't be sure if he was imagining things but he swore he started feeling like he was floating. He instantly felt compelled to close his eyes.

Fears, Fantasies & Freedom

The feeling of weightlessness was electrifying but also a little terrifying. This was no dream, or was it? No, he was definitely going up. Neil grabbed Noah's arm to keep himself grounded. Noah was saying something to him but he couldn't quite make out what it was. His grip on Noah's arm loosened and now he was sure he could hear Noah shouting, but Neil was already on his way up; no longer tethered to any earthly body. As he levitated within the light, he felt a deep sense of comfort. Noah's voice grew fainter and fainter while Neil continued his upwards journey within the light. The more Neil rose, the more he let go. He let go of all his problems and just kept floating. Eventually a deep slumber overtook Neil, his body had now gone limp as he was suspended several feet above the ground. Then just like that, he was gone.

When Neil finally opened his eyes, he was no longer floating. His eyes met the glassy black gaze of an actual alien. At least that's what Neil assumed he was staring back at. Its skin was a deep gray with an almost impossibly perfect oval-shaped head sitting on a long neck. The extraterrestrial tilted its head almost quizzically as Neil sat up on the table.

Fears, Fantasies & Freedom

"So, the Grays *are* real huh," he quips. He quickly caught himself and felt a tad embarrassed that those were his first words when meeting an extraterrestrial being. But there's no one to hear him anyway, at least no other humans. Neil looked around and counted nine other aliens in the room with him. They were tall in stature with unique wrinkles on their forehead and a bulbous head. They had no nose but two openings for nostrils and blue tongues that stuck out sometimes when they communicated with each other. Neil couldn't understand a word they said. The alien observing him carried a long silver scepter or rod that it periodically waved over Neil's body. Neil was in disbelief that he was actually experiencing this event and he closed his eyes several times, trying to wake up, because there was no way that this was not a dream. He knew he'd wanted to go to Vegas with Darnell to have a time that was 'out of this world' but this was certainly pushing it. What would he even tell Darnell when he saw him again? Would he ever see him again? Neil silently cursed himself for leaving the party to go make out with Noah. He wondered why the light didn't take Noah as well. Now he was all alone with who knows what going to who knows where.

The Grays all seem to like flowy garments that complemented their sleek body. The fabric seemed almost like a fluid, flowing and coalescing around their lean and lanky bodies.

Fears, Fantasies & Freedom

"*Mantjin,*" said the alien observing Neil. "*Chlat meko rugvan bisay.*"

"*Chlat rugvani,*" all the others seem to agree.

They gathered around Neil, some politely prodding and poking at him as they experienced interaction with a human for their first time. Or maybe this was not their first time. Neil had no idea. One of them handed him what seemed to be goblet and said, "*Mraklo*" Neil nervously laughed and sipped from the goblet so as not to be rude. A warm sensation flowed through him as he drank the contents of the goblet. The liquid was sweet, almost sickeningly so, but it wasn't unpleasant enough that Neil stopped drinking. when he was done, he held out the goblet and the Gray that first observed him took it and walked away. Soon all the Grays dispersed from around him, as they went back to whatever they were doing before he woke up. The room had massive windows that allowed Neil to see outside. The inside of the room had panels and equipment that Neil could not make heads or tails of, but the Grays seemed busy at work monitoring whatever it was they were working on. Slowly, Neil got up off the table and walked over to one of the windows to look out. He wanted to see if they were still floating above the canyon. To Neil's despair they were nowhere near Earth. They were in deep space. All he saw were stars.

"I've got to get back," he exclaimed. He turned around trying to get the Grays' attention. "I have to go home!"

"*Miqhan Xuc,*" one of them said, offering no assistance.

Neil started using his hands to accompany the message he was trying to get through, "I. Have. To. Get. Back. To Earth."

"*Miqhan Xuglivan!*" The alien responded with something that looked like what may be their species' smiles. A few Grays turned toward him and said in unison, "*Xugi xugi avliani.*" They finished with that same 'smile' the previous alien had given Neil. Still no help to get back to Earth. Neil felt defeated, but oddly, he felt no fear. There were very few things more exciting than being on an alien spaceship. Especially if they all appeared so friendly. Neil sighed and turned his attention back toward the vast windows. The starfield and constellations were totally different from anything Neil had ever seen on Earth. It was breathtaking to behold. Even with being abducted, Neil was grateful for small blessings. Neil walked back over to the table he was laying on initially to lay on it once again. He dozed off to the sounds of the aliens swaying, possibly laughing and shouting "*Chukanya!*" Maybe one day he will get back to Earth, but that day was not today.

5

Leave the Door Open

A sliver of afternoon sun peeks through the dark curtains, displaying an illuminated thin line shining on Dr. Lawson's desk. Her office is modestly furnished. Two men sit on opposite ends of a dark burgundy couch directly across from her. She leans forward, peering through spectacles at the separated couple. She quietly clears her throat then gestures with the pen in her hand, "So?"

The couple, Leon and Charles, shift in their seats uncomfortably. Neither says a word. Dr. Lawson was used to silences like this, especially in couples counseling.

She gestures with her pen and points at the older man, "Charles, do *you* think it's a good idea to host the holiday dinner this year? Since Leon doesn't seem to want to answer."

Charles sighs then answers, "I mean, I would love to do it. Matter of fact, I am doing it, but I don't want to actually do it without him. We've been planning it for months and I don't think we should just cancel those plans just because we're on a little break."

Leon pipes up, "Is it a little break?"

Fears, Fantasies & Freedom

"That's what we said, right? That's why we're here in counseling to work out whatever you think we need to work out," Charles rep

Dr. Lawson leans forward momentarily as if to interject but Leon speaks first, "Whatever *I* think we need to work out? Are you fucking kidding me Charles?"

"Alright, wait, hold up," Dr. Lawson finally intervenes, "That's important. Charles, you just said you are here to work out whatever Leon thinks you need to work out. So, don't *you* think there's anything to work on?"

Charles tilts his head to the side and purses his lips before answering, "Of course I do, that's not how I meant it. I just mean that he is the one who wanted to separate. That wasn't me. And all our friends for the past six years look forward to our holiday dinner, so I don't think they should be punished - or frankly, *I* should be punished, just because Leon wants to prove a point. I get it. We have problems, and I am willing to work on them and work on myself and whatever else he needs to feel loved and cared for. I've said all this already."

Leon delivers an eye roll and a sharp sigh then stands up.

"You see?" he begins, "He still doesn't get it! He makes it look like we got into an argument a few nights ago and I've been sleeping on the couch. Hello? We've been separated for three months and the last time we spoke before today was last week in *this* same room, at *this* same time. Why would I want to co-host a holiday dinner with him so we can pretend to be happy and paint on plastic smiles and lean into some fake life and some fucked up facade just so he doesn't feel punished? He might be fine with all the pretending and the fake bullshit but the main reason I came to this country was so that I didn't have to be fake anymore. And I'll be damned if I let him undermine my integrity."

He finishes by throwing himself back on to the couch, this time widening the already wide distance between himself and his husband.

"Alright, alright. We'll call it off," Charles relents, "Whatever you want, Leon. I just want to make you happy."

"And does that make you happy, Leon?" Dr. Lawson inquires.

Len sucks his teeth. "Listen, I'm happy if he's happy and we're happy. Whether separately or together."

"I'm not happy we're apart." Charles offers, trying to make eye contact with Leon. Leon avoids his gaze.

"I'm not happy about it either Charles," Leon says, "I love you and it pains me but it's just what we need right now. You think I don't think about you every day, miss your coffee in the morning, miss your back rubs …"

"Then just come home!" Charles exclaims.

"There are also the things that I don't miss," Leon continues, making a show of listing off items on his fingers, "Your controlling ways, your overbearingness...feeling stifled."

"Here we go again!" Charles says, rising to his feet. He takes a couple of steps towards Leon and stands in front of him. "Like, I said. I'm working on it. That's why you haven't heard from me since last week. I'm giving you your space. I'm trying to make an effort. Can't you see that?"

"Hmph," comes Leon's reply.

Charles' shoulders slump and he returns to his end of the couch. He sits down, deflated. There is silence for a beat. Dr. Lawson watches them both closely, wondering if she should let this play out or interrupt the momentary silence. Then Charles lights up.

"I'll probably call up Maggie and see if she and Paul have any holiday plans."

Maggie is Charles' ex-wife and mother to his son CJ. After the divorce she married Paul and even though Maggie and Charles were no longer together, they still shared an ever-present friendship. Maggie and Leon had developed their own friendship over the years and both couples spent quite a few holidays together.

"Maybe I can still score a piece of Maggie's peach cobbler even though we're not having the dinner this year. I'm sure gonna miss Lisa's rum cake though." Charles complains playfully.

Leon laughs at the mention of his cousin's name. "I might have to call up Maggie myself and see if she can send me a slice. Luckily, Lisa will be with me so I'm gonna have her rum cake all to myself."

Dr. Lawson finds an opening. "Well maybe in the spirit of the holidays, you both can exchange baked goodies this year," she offers.

"Maybe," says Leon quietly.

"Oh, Lisa's staying with you for the holidays?" asks Charles.

"Well not the whole time, just for a few days up until the 25th then it's back to New York."

"Well, I'm glad someone's going to be there, cause that neighborhood is a little rough," Charles says with a grimace, "Especially at this time of year..."

At this, Leon's friendly countenance dissipates and he leans away from Charles, "Thanks for your concern but I'll be fine. Nothing has happened to me in the 3 months since I've moved there. And I know it's not the white, upper-middle class side of the tracks that you're used to but I feel quite at home there. We've got the Jamaican restaurant just down the street, the Caribbean market two blocks away and plus I took three years of karate in primary school so if I need to beat a bitch down, I'll beat a bitch down."

Leon's cell phone makes a loud *ding* and he quickly checks the screen then returns the phone to his pocket.

Charles narrows his eyes, "Shouldn't your phone be off? Who's that anyway?"

Rising from her chair, Dr. Lawson speaks before Leon could answer, "That's our time, anyway. I think this week was productive. I'll see you both again, after the holidays. Maybe a little holiday cheer is just what you two need to fully assess where each of your happiness lies and what you want the next year of your lives to look like. Remember to listen to each other."

Charles rises from his seat and extends a hand toward Dr. Lawson. "Thank you, doctor. I hope you can see I'm really trying here," he says.

Dr. Lawson smiles and shakes his hand. Leon stands and they do the same. Charles heads towards the door and makes his exit. Leon watches him leave while silently wondering what new surprises the holiday season will bring now that he's separated from Charles. Leon walks to the door and stops in the doorway, turning to speak to Dr. Lawson.

"As always, Dr. Lawson, thank you for your time. Should I leave the door open or close it behind me?"

"Leave it open," Dr. Lawson replies, "I have another client right now. Thanks, Leon."

Leon waves back as he leaves, "Happy Holidays!"

✵ ✵ ✵

The smell of 'high grade' fills the air as Leon passes a joint to his best friend Brett as they sit on the couch in Leon's living room. Leon's favorite cousin Lisa is also there, sitting on the floor with her back leaning against the coffee table.

"So, this is a done deal? By next year I'll be able to walk into a store and point out your necklaces and smugly say, "My best friend designed these, I'll have the gold *and* the silver!" says Brett between puffs of the joint.

Leon laughs and says, "Well it's not a done deal yet. I have one last meeting with these white people to settle on the pieces of the collection they want to carry. But if everything goes well, you'll be seeing my jewelry in boutiques and stores all over. From here in Baltimore, down to DC and even Virginia. I'm really keeping my fingers crossed that everything goes well."

"It's going to go great," Lisa chimes in, taking the joint from Brett. "I'm so proud of you cuz. My cousin is gonna be a big-time designer. Soon get rich and switch."

Leon guffaws loudly. "I don't know about all that. But I'm just happy it's all coming together. I couldn't have gotten this far without the love and support you both give me. You both made me believe that I could really do this."

Brett reaches over and gives Leon a hug. "It's all you Leon," he says. "I'm always so impressed by your strength and your growth, even in the face of some hard choices and tough decisions."

Fears, Fantasies & Freedom

"That's part of why I knew I had to break things off with Charles, you know?" Leon replies. "I feel like I really let the last six years pass me by. I just had all these ideas in my head about my art and my business but I wasn't motivated enough to make shit happen. Now, I'm almost 30 and I'm like, 'Fuck, what have I done with my life?' The moment I shacked up with Charles, my entire life became all about him. It was his life, his home, his parties, his friends, his business and I got so caught up in it all, that I lost myself at some point along the way."

Lisa reaches across and places a hand on Leon's knee, "Well we all get a little lovestruck sometimes. Nothing to be ashamed of. He's your husband. You wanted to play the part of the dutiful spouse and you did it well. And who knows if this is the end. Charles surely still loves you."

"And he love that white man too, don't let the new address fool you. Leon will be back over in that house in no time," Brett teases, laughing.

Leon laughs while playfully pushing Brett, "No, I will not. Of course, I still love Charles, I probably won't ever stop loving him. I can't say definitively that our marriage is over but I need us to feel like it is. This break and separation have to hold some weight. I have to step out on my own two feet and do the damn thing and he needs to be able to understand that he doesn't own me and we are both free agents. I even told him that he can date other people."

"And what did he say to that?" Lisa questions.

"He said he already found what he needed so he didn't need to go searching for it."

"Aww, that's so sweet." says Brett mockingly.

Changing the subject, Leon replies, "Not as sweet as Lisa's rum cake is gonna be. I'm so glad I have you two over so we can do a lil' holiday shindig. Just the three of us. Like how it used to be when we just moved to America like a decade ago."

"It's cute that you changed the subject but I'mma bring it back," says Lisa, "How did Charles feel about not doing the big holiday dinner this year?"

"He wasn't too thrilled."

"I bet," Brett exclaims, "Damn I'm gonna miss Maggie's peach cobbler this year though."

Leon laughs at this. "That's what I said! You know, our therapist recommended that Charles and I exchange baked treats this year. I give him a slice of Lisa's cake and he'll give me a slice of Maggie's cobbler. In the spirit of holiday cheer!"

"It's still so crazy to me that Charles would want to spend the holidays with his ex-wife and her husband or that Maggie would want to spend it with her lonely gay ex-husband. Those two really are a special case. I know I wouldn't be caught dead spending the holidays with any of my exes," Brett states incredulously.

"Well, Brett honey, none of your flings have ever lasted long enough to make it past Thanksgiving." Lisa says with a snort.

"Girl, don't come for me," Brett retorts, "I did not send for you tonight."

"Brett, pass me the spliff," Leon requests, "Let's finish smoking and start getting some stuff ready for this dinner in a few days. You know we have to season the meat from now so it can marinate in all those spices and juices and I want to make the sorrel from tonight so we don't have to think about it on the day."

"And I'm so ready to pop open the jar of fruits I've been soaking in rum since a year ago. This cake is about to be everything," Lisa says. The three friends get up from the couch and floor respectively and head into the kitchen to prepare for the holiday festivities.

✳ ✳ ✳

Charles is sitting at the table in his living room, with a glass of wine on the table in front of him. In the kitchen next to the dining room, a middle-aged woman busies herself at the kitchen counter, poring a glass of wine for herself. An expensive handbag sits on the dining table across from Charles.
Charles looks a little sad as he takes big gulps from the wine glass. Usually hanging out with his ex-wife and best friend, Maggie would bring him a lot of cheer, but his current situation and separation has caused him to be in a bit of a funk.

"I'm sorry it's just me," Maggie says, "Paul and his brothers are spending the afternoon with their parents. Since you canceled your big holiday dinner, he thought he finally should take the opportunity to go down to Richmond this year since they've been inviting him for the last four years."

"Then how come you're here Mags? You didn't want to see the in-laws?" Charles asks.

"Now Chuckie, you know I've never really been a fan of my in-laws. Plus, how could I leave my best friend all alone on Christmas?"

"My husband left me all alone," Charles says, feeling sorry for himself.

Maggie sighs. "You're not all alone. I'm here."

Fears, Fantasies & Freedom

"The only constant in my life. Why did we ever get divorced again?" Charles questions.

"Because you wanted to be free. And I wanted you to be happy." Maggie ends her activity at the kitchen counter and walks over to the dining room table with a bottle. She refills Charles' glass and embraces him. Charles sighs and leans into the hug.

"How are you holding up?" Maggie asks

"I don't know," Charles responds, "It's just... I feel like I'm a failure."

"A failure?" Maggie repeats. She takes a seat across from Charles. "Come on, you have a very successful real estate company, a son in the middle of grad school, this big house, and a couple of cars sitting out front. And you still look good, I'm sure you could go out there and snag a cutie whenever you like."

"Mags, I've already got one failed marriage with you, a dead partner with Kofi and am now in the middle of another failing marriage. This one, not even lasting a full three years."

"First of all, our marriage was not a failure," Maggie remarks, "It produced Charles Jr. So, we have something good to show for it. We also had lots of love and laughter and great times, even if our bedroom was rarely active. We developed a bond and a friendship that will never go away. I wouldn't trade those 15 years for anything."

Charles looks at Maggie. Her kind eyes were what drew him to her when they started dating all those years ago. He was grateful to still have her in his life.

"That's really nice of you to say but the way I see it, I took an innocent 19-year-old girl from her home with her life still ahead of her. And because I was so afraid to be true to myself, I married her, knocked her up and subjected her to 15 years of a dead bed marriage. Then we got a divorce so I could be happy. Right? Where did that get me? I met and fell in love with Kofi and in six years he was taken from me in a car accident. I couldn't even protect him. Then my own son stopped talking to me after all I had done to take care of him. And now my second marriage is down the shitter."

Maggie takes a swig of her wine, "You've got to stop beating yourself up over Kofi. That wasn't your fault. You couldn't have predicted it; you couldn't have stopped it. It was out of your hands. And as for CJ. He is our son. *Your* son. It might be a little rocky now but I promise you it will get better."

"I don't know Maggie. I tried to be a great dad bu-"

"And you were!" Maggie interrupts.

"Was I? My own son hasn't called me since last Christmas. He didn't show up to mine and Leon's wedding two and a half years ago and where is he this year? I haven't heard from him and it's Christmas again. I'm sure he called you this morning."

Maggie grimaces a little and sighs, "Yes, I did speak with him. But Chuckie you gotta remember, this is a two-way street. Did you try calling CJ today or any time over the past year?"

"I'm his father! I shouldn't have to chase him down," Charles exclaims, "He keeps trying to bring up all these non-existent issues that I apparently need to take accountability for. I wish I could've said the same shit to my father. Accountability, please!"

"Maybe you should listen to him. I'm not going to get involved," Maggie says, resigned. She shakes her head and holds up her hands. "You're both your own men and stubborn as hell. But if you truly want to rebuild the relationship with your son you seriously have to listen to what he's saying to you and stop treating him like a child."

There is a ring from Charles' pocket. He pauses drinking and answers the phone. "Hello. Surprised to see you calling."

Maggie signals to him and mouths, *"Who is it?"*

Charles whispers back while covering the phone speaker, "It's Leon."

Fears, Fantasies & Freedom

He turns his attention back to the phone and engages in conversation. "Wait, so what happened? Your oven? Oh shit. Well, I mean, you could use mine if you're desperate. No, I didn't mean it that way. So, what are you going to do? You should come. Of course, bring them too. I'm here with Mags. Ok, see you soon. Bye." He hangs up the phone and places it on the table.

"What was that all about?" Maggie asks.

"Apparently, Leon's oven at his new apartment stopped working just as Lisa was about to bake the rum cake," Charles replies, trying but failing to hide his excitement. "Please set three extra places at the table. My husband is coming home."

Two hours later, there is a grand gathering in Charles' dining room. Leon, Brett, Lisa, Maggie and Charles sit around the table laughing, eating, drinking and conversing with much merriment. It is around the end of dinner and each of them is busy digging into some decadent dessert.

"Baybee! Maggie honey! That peach cobbler hits the sweet spot every time," declares Bett, between bites of the cobbler.

"No lies detected there," agrees Lisa, "This is simply heaven Maggie."

"I'm really glad we didn't have to go a year without your famous rum cake Lisa. It truly is to die for," compliments Maggie.

"Well, I'm just glad I got to spend the holiday with my husband," says Charles. He reaches across the table and grabs Leon's hand.

Leon flashes a smile and says, "Me too Charles, this was really great."

Leon's phone vibrates and he removes his hand from under Charles' hand to check his phone then quickly puts it back in his pocket. Charles notices and narrows his eyes while shifting in his seat.

"Y'all really came through when we were in a jam," Lisa says, "It was great to bring our dishes together and have a good-ass holiday spread."

"And I know there weren't the thirty extra people you usually have here annually for this dinner, but this intimate setting was just what we needed," Maggie says looking at Charles.

"Hmm, maybe we do something similar next year, right Leon? Maybe start a new tradition? If that's what you want of course," Charles says, reaching out for Leon's hand.

"Maybe," Leon says, ignoring Charles' hand. He takes a sip from his cup and looks off into the distance pensively.

Fears, Fantasies & Freedom

"When I was growing up, Christmastime was only cold on TV," Leon begins, "There's no winter where I'm from. No snow, no white Christmas, no chestnuts roasting on any fireplaces, no chimneys for St. Nick to sneak down, matter of fact we never thought Santa Claus came to the tropics. I don't think there was ever one standard Christmas tradition that our family observed.

"The activities changed every year. There were years where we went to the beach or gave the house a new coating of paint. I remember we would also go to Grand Market on Christmas Eve night, it felt like the entire country was shopping in your town. The hustle and bustle to get last-minute items and unique wares seemed to draw everyone to the streets. I would get lost in the sounds and smells and sights. When I was really young, we would sometimes go see the Jonkonnu parade. Scared the living shit out of me: Pitchy-Patchy, Cow-head, Belly Woman all in their masks and flamboyant costumes. A sight to behold for sure. Exciting but terrifying.

"When I was a little older, family members from America and Canada would visit and bring us all sorts of gifts and goodies from 'foreign.' And depending on the year we would have big family gatherings and even big extended family trips in some years.

"When I moved here a decade ago, that was the first time I ever experienced a cold Christmas, so that was new and exciting. It's not lost on me that in the ten years I've lived here, I've only experienced one white Christmas. Fucking TV lied to me.

"The last six years however, Charles and I have committed to hosting the lavish Christmas dinner. It took months to plan and there were always so many moving pieces and it was a lot of work. It became our tradition, though to be honest it was Charles' tradition that I got roped into doing. As far as I know he'd been doing this for years before he met me. Anyway, I'm rambling at this point. Too much spiked eggnog," Leon laughed a little at this.

"My point is: doing this impromptu, intimate dinner tonight was just the change of pace I needed," finished Leon, before taking another bite of the rum cake.

"Agreed. This was great, I reckon I had way more fun than Paul had down in Richmond," declares Maggie, "I know I'm about to get home and have him talking my ear off, complaining about his mama. She can be a real tough bitch, when she's ready. That's why I keep my distance." Maggie finishes with a dramatic flourish while rising from her seat.

"You about to head home, Mags?" Charles asks.

"Yeah, I think it's about that time." Maggie responds.

Brett stands up and stretches, yawning loudly, "About time for me to bounce too. Thank you all for the good time, good food and good company."

"Always a pleasure having you over," Charles says. They all stand and exchange gigs as Maggie and Brett depart.

After they leave, Lisa also stands and picks up her purse. "This is my last night before I head back to New York so I'm thinking of going out after this," she says, "They're having a show at the Soundstage if you all are interested."

"I'll pass," Charles says, "I'm beat. Leon?"

"I'll pass too cuz, I'm so full I'm about to pass out right here," Leon says, rubbing his stomach.

"Ooh, not the itis," Lisa laughs.

"Leon, the guest bedroom is prepared if you feel like you want to lie down," Charles offers.

"No thanks," Leon declines, "I think I'm going to head home. I literally only live 15 minutes away."

"Alright, I'll see you next time Charles," Lisa says, giving a departing hug, "Leon, I'll see you in the morning. My car is here."

"See you in the morning. Be safe! Text me when you get there," Leon says giving her an embrace.

Fears, Fantasies & Freedom

"Will do," Lisa waves as she closes the front door behind her.

There is silence for a beat before Charles speaks. "And then there were two…"

Leon looks down at his phone, almost impatiently and responds, "For now."

"Come on," Charles entreats, "You don't have to leave. This is your home. Just stay."

"Baby, this hasn't been my home for three months now," Leon dismissively says.

"But it's cold outside, maybe just sit by the fire for a -" Charles begins.

"I'll get warm at home," Leon curtly interrupts.

"It's so late too, you know it's sketchy where you live. I don't want you in any danger."

Leon rolls his eyes, "I'm sure I'll be just fine. It's Christmas, you know."

"I'm aware. We had such a lovely night tonight. I ju-"

"And I don't want to spoil it."

"Listen, I jus-" Charles pleads.

"Oh look!" cries Leon, looking down at his phone, "My car is here. Gotta go!" He reaches out to give Charles a departing hug.

Charles receives the hug then leans in for a kiss. Leon rejects him. Charles, quite stung, apologizes, "Oh. Sorry. Merry Christmas, Leon."

"Merry Christmas, Charles." With another quick wave, Leon departs, closing the front door behind him.

Fears, Fantasies & Freedom

Leon gets home a little after midnight. He fumbles with his keys as he opens the door. Once inside, he makes his way through the dark living room and enters the kitchen. He then pours himself a cup of water from the refrigerator then returns to the living room. He takes a sip then lounges on the couch, still in the dark. He fishes his phone from his pocket and spends a few moments scrolling through social media. He then gets up and turns on the living room light before returning to the couch to continue scrolling on his phone. A sudden but soft thud comes from behind the couch. Leon barely looks up to acknowledge the sound. A few moments later Leon hears a loud clatter from behind the couch and he leaps into action.

"What the fuck!?"

A masked assailant in all-black clothing jumps from behind the couch brandishing a crowbar and lunges at Leon. Leon sidesteps the intruder and follows up with a solid strike to the abdomen leaving him gasping for air, and the crowbar clattering to the floor. Seeing Leon readying for another attack, the intruder intercepts him by tackling him to the ground. The two men wrestle on the ground for a while before the intruder gets the upper hand and delivers two strikes to Leon's face.

"Get offa me!" Leon shouts.

The trespasser continues to deliver more blows to Leon's head and face as Leon struggles to be free. The intruder eventually manages to get Leon into a headlock, pinning him to the ground. Leon gasps for air, clawing at the bicep that threatens to crush his windpipe. He spots the crowbar just a few inches away from his hand. Still struggling to wrest free of the encroacher, Leon inches closer to the crowbar. His vision begins to go dark. Then suddenly his fingers feel the cold metal. He clasps his hand around the rod and with everything inside him, he swings it behind him, connecting with the intruder's head. The invader lets go of Leon and instead grabs his head in pain, running toward the front door as drops of blood follow him in his flight. He throws the door open and exits, leaving the door open behind him.

Leon is still trying to catch his breath and sobs. "Fuck, fuck, fuck, fuck." He reaches for his phone and dials a number. He holds the phone to his ear while he waits for it to pick up, tears streaming down his face. The call picks up.

"Hello," says a voice.

"Charles! I need you!"

✵ ✵ ✵

Fears, Fantasies & Freedom

Three weeks after the break-in, Leon and Charles meet with Dr. Lawson for their counselling session. Both men sit very close to each other on the couch and hold hands as they talk to Dr. Lawson.

"Well how long have you two been like this?" Dr. Lawson probes.

"Like what?" Leon asks.

"This… close," replies Dr. Lawson, gesturing to both men.

"Around three weeks now. Ever since the break-in," Charles responds.

"And Leon how do you feel about that?" Dr. Lawson inquires, peering over her spectacles.

Leon sighs. "The break-in was the most terrifying thing to ever happen to me. I'm just glad I made it out alive. I gave a statement to the cops. Described the guy as best as I could. I couldn't even see his face so I didn't give them much to work with aside from his height and build. To be honest though, I'm still shook up. I've been having these dreams."

"What kind of dreams?" Dr. Lawson asks.

"In the dreams, it's like I recognize my attacker," Leon says, "But every time I wake up, I forget it. It's been driving me crazy. But I've been trying to just move forward and not actively dwell on that night, so the dreams can go away."

"I offered for him to sleep over at my place as long as he wanted but he insists on staying in that apartment," Charles says, rubbing Leon's shoulder.

"I'll be fine, Charles."

"So how are you feeling about Charles in all this?" Dr. Lawson poses to Leon.

Leon thinks for a moment before he replies. "Well, we're the closest we've been these past three weeks than we've been the entire three and a half months we've been separated. He's really shown up, you know.

"Charles what about you?" Dr. Lawson asks, "How do you feel about all this?"

"I'm just so lucky to have my husband with me. I'll do anything to protect him and keep him safe. This whole ordeal really shook me though. I just wish I was there." Charles answers.

"I see," says Dr. Lawson, "So, what does this mean for your relationship? Your marriage?"

Charles pipes up, "Well we talk on the phone every day and I see him maybe 5 times a week now so I'd like to think we're moving in the right direction. Hopefully, he's back under my roof by Spring, or even next month."

Dr. Lawson looks at Leon who had let go of Charles' hand to scratch an itch on his face. "Leon, same question."

Fears, Fantasies & Freedom

Leon seems to hesitate. He opens his mouth to speak then appears to change his mind. He takes a second, breathes, then tries again. "Well, Charles has been a god-send. As well as my other friends, old and new. I'm so grateful for them all. Charles slept in the hospital with me the night of the attack and Brett and Lisa were there for me the next day when they discharged me. Lisa even missed her flight back to New York and extended her stay an extra week. So, everyone has been mighty supportive."

Dr. Lawson notes how carefully Leon chose his words. She wondered what that meant for the couple's relationship moving forward. "What about the marriage aspect? Are there plans to rekindle the spark? Has any rekindling already begun?"

"If you mean, have we slept together, then no," Leon says quickly.

"Baby steps, baby steps," Charles soothes, "After he moves back in, that will be a natural occurrence. Right now, my only concern is making sure he is protected and safe from harm. I couldn't bear the thought of losing him like that."

Leon slightly pulls away from Charles, his face sports a frown. "Charles I never once said I was moving back in with you. Why do you keep saying that?"

"I just thought… After everything, you were ready to come back. Ready for me to keep you safe."

"Let me interject here," Dr. Lawson jumps in. "Leon, so are you saying there is no hope of reconciliation?"

Leon shakes his head, "I'm not saying that. The door is still open, it always was. I wouldn't be here with you if I didn't want to fight for this marriage. Nevertheless, just because that incident happened, it doesn't mean that it suddenly made everything better in our marriage. We still need the time and space to figure out what the hell we're doing. Nothing got fixed."

"I just want to be able to safeguard you and that's easier if we're under the same roof," Charles insists.

"That's fine. I get what you're saying. But Charles, you have to realize I'm not Kofi. I don't want to be smothered because of a tragic experience in your past. I'm Leon, not Kofi."

This was a new wrinkle that Dr. Lawson had not heard before. "Who's Kofi?" she asked.

"He was my partner before I met Leon," Charles replies, "He was my first serious relationship after my divorce from Maggie. I lost him in a car accident."

Dr. Lawson removes her glasses. "I'm sorry for your loss, Charles. Do you think you might be projecting some of that trauma and insecurity onto Leon? This incessant need to protect him, do you think that stems from this tragedy?"

"I'm sure that may be a factor. But who says that's a bad thing? What's so wrong with wanting him to be safe at all times? I have a reason to feel the way I feel. Kofi died. Leon got attacked in his 'home.' My behavior is perfectly rational," Charles opines.

"Not if it involves calling my friends to find out where I am when you can't get me, or keeping tabs on where I'm going and who I'm talking to, or trying to control and manipulate me overtly or covertly for your own means," Leon says. The distance on the couch between them slowly grows wider.

"I know Leon. And I promised you that all that obsessive, controlling mess was done," Charles admits. "I can't apologize enough. I didn't even realize what I was doing half the time. But can't you see why I find it so important that you're safe? You could have died that night."

"I understand Charles. I really do."

Charles appears to think for a while; formulating a plan. "What about getting a security system? Some alarms, a few cameras around the apartment. Like real good high-tech stuff. I'll pay for it. You wouldn't have to spend a dime."

Leon is unsure. "Hmm… I dunno. Cameras though? It kinda feels… I dunno."

"Hear me out," Charles holds up his palms. "Next time if anything like that were to happen, then the camera footage would have all the information for the cops. And you could even connect it to your phone so you can always keep abreast of what's happening in that apartment. So, if you're not willing to move back in with me, then the least I can do is this."

Leon mulls over this for a while. It seems like Charles would not take no for an answer and he probably could benefit from having more security in his apartment. "Okay. I concede. It would make me feel safer."

"Oh, have we reached a compromise?" Dr. Lawson asks.

Leon nods. "I think so, doctor."

"This is great to see. Good work to both of you. I think we've all but run out of time so I'll see you both at our next appointment."

Charles stands and stretches then reaches out to shake Dr. Lawson's hand, "Thank you, see you next time."

Leon does the same then both men exit, seemingly set on a new path.

Leon sits on the couch next to Brett as they experiment with the new security upgrades in Leon's apartment. There were small cameras by the front door and in different rooms of the apartment.

Fears, Fantasies & Freedom

"This is actually pretty cool. You can see the kitchen, the living room, the hallway as well as the front and back doors," Brett says as he holds Leon's phone.

"I know, it's like my very own smart house. The front door camera actually makes a loud whistling noise to scare off intruders and porch pirates."

"I need to get me one of those," notes Brett, "There's some sneaky bitch in my neighborhood making off with my Amazon packages. I'm 'bout to pull up on they ass."

Leon chuckles. "I know that's right! Now I can monitor that shit from my phone. The future is now."

Leon's phone dings in Brett's hand. Brett's expression transforms gradually from one of curiosity, to one of amazement then to that of excitement as he reads the incoming message.

"Gimme that!" Leon commands. He reaches for his phone as Brett holds it high, reading the message out loud, "*Are you up right now? Kissy face emoji.* Who the fuck is Rob? And why does he want to know if you're up right now?"

Leon answers sheepishly, "Rob is my friend. Gimme that!" He snatches the phone from Brett's grasp.

"How many of your friends send you kissy face emojis?"

"The ones who care to kiss me."

"How long has this been going on?" Brett asks incredulously. "I'm your best friend and I ain't never heard of no Rob. Is this who you've been texting all the time? Don't think Lisa and I haven't noticed you smiling at your phone and discreetly sliding it back in your pocket."

"No, I do not," Leon lies.

"Oh yes, you do," Brett counters, "Come on, tell me more about this Rob. Is he hot? Are you boning? Does Charles know?"

Leon sighs and concedes, "Yes, no and no. And you can't say a word. I haven't mentioned it because I don't know where it's going yet. We've been texting for a couple months now and we've been out on maybe four dates. In public. That's all. It's nothing to talk about yet."

Brett claps his hands and laughs loudly. "But look at you! Getting kissy emojis from suitors. I've got to shout it to the rooftops." He jumps off the couch and races to the door, swinging it open.

"Brett, no!" Leon shouts.

A loud siren suddenly pierces the air and Brett slams the door shut, covering his ears. Leon presses some commands on his phone and the alarm stops immediately.

"What the fuck was that?" Brett crudely questions.

Fears, Fantasies & Freedom

"That was the security system you nincompoop. You have to disarm it before opening the door or else the alarm goes off. Let me just send them a report from the app that everything is fine."

"That's going to become kind of a bother, don't you think?" Brett asks, retaking his seat on the couch.

"I'll get used to it," Leon shrugs, "Better safe than sorry right."

"What I wish was that that alarm summoned a pizza guy. I am starving." Brett says, rubbing his stomach dramatically.

"Me too. I was going to cook tonight but then you came over, and you know how lazy I get when guests come over," Leon chuckles.

"Okay, why don't you find something online for us to eat and I'll find something on TV for us to watch," Brett suggests.

They spend the next few minutes perusing takeout menus and channel guides until the doorbell suddenly rings.

"You expecting somebody?" Brett inquires.

"Nope, wonder who it is." Leon gets up and disarms the security system then opens the door. Standing there is Charles with two large boxes of pizza in tow. "Charles, what are you doing here?" Leon asks surprised.

Fears, Fantasies & Freedom

"I was in the neighborhood and I thought to myself, why don't I just pick up some of that hot pizza from around the corner. I know you love their pies so I thought why don't I visit my husband and drop off some food? Can I come in?" Charles asks while pushing the pizza boxes through the doorway.

"Sure. Come in. You actually turned up just in time, we were about to order some food." Leon says, welcoming Charles.

"Charles! You're a lifesaver!" Brett declares, "I'm fucking famished."

"That's what I like to hear," Charles says taking a seat, "Come on, dig in."

"You don't have to ask me twice," Brett says, taking a bite of pizza. He continues speaking with the food in his mouth, "So Charlie, what's up with you? What you got going on?"

"Ah, I just closed on a good property yesterday. It's one of those blocks of rowhouses just north of Patterson Park. It doesn't look like much now, but once we turn it around and redevelop it, everybody is going to want a piece."

"Oh, good for you Charles, more blacks and browns displaced to make way for one of your ugly-ass condos. Love that for you. Not!" Brett snarks.

"Oh, it's not like that al-" Charles starts.

"I'm sure it is," Brett interrupts, "But that's what you do so I don't expect any less...or any better of you." Brett takes another slice of pizza from the box then chuckles. "I'm just fucking around with you Charlie boy. Your good white wealth got us this pizza and it feels good in my tummy so you won't catch me complaining. At least not tonight." With this, Brett devours his pizza slice.

"Brett, lay off of him," Leon chides, "I do have an announcement to make, since both of you are here."

"Is that so?" Charles says, sitting up in his seat.

"Oh, this is exciting," Brett says.

Leon begins, "I was going to wait to share this but…"

"OMG!" Brett exclaims.

"The deal went through! Starting next month, my jewelry will be available in stores all across Maryland, the District and Virginia. And if it goes well moving forward, we might be available in stores up and down the Eastern Seaboard by the end of the year!" Leon announces.

Brett jumps off the couch and goes to hug Leon, "That's amazing! Congrats! I knew you had it in you! It's only a matter of time before you take over the world."

"Congratulations babe! I'm so proud of you. This is what you deserve," Charles says.

"We have to celebrate!" Brett declares.

Leon begins walking toward the kitchen, "I do have a bottle of champagne in the fridge. Let me go get it and a few glasses." Leon leaves then returns with the bottle and a few champagne flutes.

Charles offers up a toast, "Let's raise our glasses to success! To Leon!"

"To Leon!" Brett repeats

"To me!" Leon agrees.

***

"It's all just been so good. It worked out perfectly. It's been almost a month since the incident now and he and I have really gotten so much closer. I feel a reconciliation is right around the corner."

Charles and Maggie are sitting in Charles' dining room catching up on the latest events in each other's lives. Charles is in a great mood and Maggie is vibing off his energy.

"I'm so happy to hear that," says Maggie, "You know I've always been rooting for you two. How is he holding up now since the break-in? That neighborhood is kinda shifty. Is he thinking of moving back in with you?"

"I really hope so. But I'm not trying to push him away again by being too overbearing. I feel safer knowing he's got the security system all set up in his apartment. That's been doing a lot to assuage my anxiety."

"Oh, that's perfect!" Maggie beams, "The emergency team will be over there straight away if any shifty, shaky shit rears its ugly head."

"I'll be there quicker than any of them ever would be," Charles says forebodingly.

"What d'you mean by that?" Maggie asks, looking hard at Charles.

"Well, I paid for the system Mags," Charles shrugs.

"Okay. Yeah, I know that, but why would you get there fas- Wait a minute? Chuckie don't tell me…"

"Tell you what?"

"Do you have access to his security system?" Maggie challenges.

"Of course, I do." Charles says matter-of-factly, "Why would I pay for something I couldn't control?"

"Have you thought this through Chuckie?"

"Not much to think through now, is there?"

Maggie stands up and begins pacing. The magnitude of what Charles had done was beginning to dawn on her. "I beg to disagree," she says, "Does he know that you have access to his security system?"

"I haven't explicitly said so, but I'm sure he must assume," Charles responds.

"So, you haven't said a word to him about it?"

"Well, no, but don't sound so scandalized Mags. It's not like I've been spying on him," Charles scoffs.

"You haven't?"

Charles pauses before answering. His eyes meet the floor as he says, "Well… there was that one time I -"

"CHARLES! ARE YOU SERIOUS RIGHT NOW?" Maggie shouts. "Isn't this the exact reason why you're separated right now? He feels trapped! Watched! Controlled! By you! Do you really want to jeopardize your relationship like this?"

"I'm not jeopardizing shit Maggie!" says Charles, raising his voice. "I'm keeping him safe. I have to."

"Chuckie, I assure you that this will not end well. This is the same shit all over again."

"What do you mean this is the same shit?"

"Because you don't listen, Chuckie," Maggie scolds, "Why do you think CJ stopped contacting you? You were so tough on him growing up. It was your way or the highway. And being our only kid, he had to take the brunt of your controlling ways. There was no other buffer.

"After the divorce, you became more distant from him since you were so caught up in your relationship with Kofi. After Kofi died, you tried to reinsert yourself back into CJ's life, trying to control him and his life choices when you had already missed out on pivotal periods during his adolescence. He was a young man now, off to college and you never took the time to listen to him and reason with him and rebuild that relationship out of love.

"It was all control again. And to him, you did not deserve a say in his life or his choices, because you were only doing it from a place of control. He ran to Chicago because he felt trapped here by you. Now you're doing the same thing to your husband. You have to get some help, Charles, this is not okay."

"Wow!" Charles exclaimed in disbelief. "So, you really think it is all my fault?"

"Well, whose fault is it then? Take some damn accountability."

"So, everything is my fault. Thanks, that made me feel so much better. I already felt like shit for destroying *our* marriage, which obviously was my fault. And I guess everything else is my fault too: Leon, CJ...Kofi."

Maggie shoots Charles a withering look, "Chuck I never fucking said that. Have some dignity, have some self-respect. How you've made yourself out to be a victim in this situation is the epitome of your controlling ways."

Fears, Fantasies & Freedom

"Maggie, what am I supposed to do?" Charles questions.

Maggie takes a breath before answering. "You remember when you came to me, fifteen years into our marriage, to tell me that you were gay? You told me you had been living a lie for so long and that I didn't deserve that and I deserved to know the truth. By that point, we had gone over two years without you touching me. Your announcement wasn't really a surprise to me, I had already guessed the obvious at that point. But you know what still stands out in my mind when I think of that day?"

"What's that?" asks Charles.

"You said you wanted to be free. To experience real freedom. The world was changing and you wanted to live your truth and be free. I could never stand in the way of that. We all want to be free. That is what Leon wants, Chuckie. To be free."

"Are you saying I should…?"

"I'm saying you should fix your shit," Maggie finishes decisively. She grabs her handbag from off the table, gives Charles a wave and exits.

Charles sighs and hangs his head as the front door shuts behind Maggie. Charles stands a and paces around the dimly lit room. Maggie just didn't understand how much he needed to protect Leon. No one understands. Only he could really keep Leon secure. Eventually Leon will be back under his roof and he won't even need that security system in his apartment. He just has to bide his time. Charles' cellphone makes a loud alert and lights up from the dining room table. Charles recognizes that alert and rushes to pick up his phone. "Shit! It's Leon's security system. Why did the alarm get tripped? I have to call him." Charles dials a number on his phone and waits as the phone rings. It goes to voicemail.

"Come on Leon, pick up!" He tries the number again. It goes to voicemail again. "Goddammit Leon, why won't you answer the phone? Ok let me just check something…" He studies his phone intently, swiping back and forth. "So, it looks like the breach came from the back door. Let me just gain access to that back door camera and I can just check to see if he's safe. Wait…who the hell is that?" Charles looks at his phone in horror.

"That can't be-? Shit! He's in danger! I have to get over there." Charles runs to the door, grabs his coat from the coat stand and exits in haste.

Charles arrives at Leon's apartment in less than 15 minutes and starts banging on the front door.

"Leon! Leon! Are you okay? Please open up. Please tell me if you're okay. Leon!"

The door swings open and Leon stands in the doorway wearing a baby blue robe. He has a look of confusion on his face. Behind Leon stands another man, wearing nothing but boxers. But Charles only has eyes for Leon and pays no attention to the other man in the dwelling. Leon pulls his robe tight and questions, "Charles? What are you doing here? What's with all the fuss this late at night?"

"I thought you were in danger. I came over as soon as I could to save you," Charles says, breathing heavily. Leon looks even more confused now, "You thought I was in-? What? How-?"

Charles steps forward trying to force himself through the doorway as he speaks, "The alarm went off and I panicked and I came as soon-" He stops speaking as he finally notices the other scantily clad man standing in the opening.
"Who's that?" Charles asks, scorn dripping from his lips.
The man steps from behind Leon and holds out his hand in greeting. Leon speaks up.

"Rob, this is Charles...my husband I told you about. Charles, Rob. He's a... friend."

Rob his still holding out his hand in greeting and says to Charles, "Nice to meet you man. It's a little awkward meeting like this, I suppose. But great to see you in the flesh." Charles' face contorts into disgust and he looks down at Rob's extended hand, then back to his face, then to Leon. He is dumbfounded. "Gr-gr-great to meet me in the flesh? Leon, what's going on here?"

Rob finally drops his hand and backs away sheepishly. He turns from the doorway and says, "Leon, I'm gon' get dressed."
Charles pushes past Leon and barrels into the living room, seething. "Leon, who the fuck is that? I need answers."

"Please calm down Charles and stop yelling inside my house," Leon replies, rolling his eyes.

"Don't tell me what to do. Answer my question!" Charles growls.

Leon casually shuts the front door and takes his time as he goes and sits on the couch. "He's someone I've been casually seeing for a little while now."

"Someone you've been seeing? Someone you've been seeing!" Charles shouts. "I'm so fucking confused right now. Someone you've been seeing? How? Then what the fuck were the last few weeks? I thought we were trying to work on our shit. Get our shit back together. Like it used to be. And you've been fucking some other guy 'named Rob' this entire time! This must be a fucking joke."

"Like it used to be?" asks Leon, raising his voice. "I don't want what we used to have Charles! That's the whole fucking point! That's why we're separated. What we used to be was toxic and controlling and manipulative. That's what we used to be and that's what I no longer want. I keep saying that but you never listen. And for the record, I haven't slept with Rob. Yes, we've been communicating for a number of weeks now, but this is the first time he's ever been to my house."

"And that's supposed to make me feel better?" Charles counters. "We've been going to counselling, I've been actively taking steps to do better. I've showed up for you time and time again. And this is how you repay me? After everything I've done for you?"

"Everything you've done for me?"

Fears, Fantasies & Freedom

"YES! Everything I've done for you!" Charles yells, "I gave you a goddamn life! I took you out of your little third-world island life and showed you real luxury. First class life, the best parties, the best people, real power, real opulence. You never had to work. You were given everything. I fucking married you! Gave you the path to citizenship in this country of my own free will and you question everything I've done for you?"

Leon finally stands, he storms over to Charles and gets in his face, "I never asked for any of it! NONE OF IT!" he screams. He takes a breath and turns his back to Charles before continuing, "Not the money, not the luxury and certainly not the fucking green card. I knew it! I knew you would hold it over my head, knowing how vulnerable a position I'm in. We have our final interview coming up this summer and I really worried that you would try to do something to screw this up for me. This is how you control and manipulate people Charles, and I can't do it anymore. Go ahead! Call immigration, call ICE. Tell them I fucked someone else and our marriage was a fraud. Go on! Six years together, almost married for three, and this is the type of shit you would pull."

Fears, Fantasies & Freedom

Charles lets out a dark chuckle which transforms his face into a disquieting grin. "So, this is how you behave, when you get caught in the act, huh? Man, what a putz I am. All the shit I have to put up with and this is the-"

"All the shit you've put up with?" Leon interrupts. His nose flared and tears welled up in his eyes as he tried to get his temper under control. "I emigrated from a country where it was extremely dangerous to be myself. I worked hard, got a scholarship and I earned my way into a university in this country. You think I don't know the shit your neighbors and some of your white, rich friends say.

"When we started dating, I was only 23 and had just graduated university. You were a successful entrepreneur in his late forties with a lot of money. The looks, the whispers, the snickers. He's a gold-digger, trafficking victim, user, dirty immigrant. Do you think I enjoyed being paraded around galas and parties on your arm like a trophy? To them I wasn't even a trophy, I was your toy. To use and abuse as you see fit. And I stuck through all of that, not because I wanted your wealth, not because I wanted status, not for a fucking green card. I did it because I loved you."

Leon plants himself back on the couch and turns away from Charles. Silence descends on the scene. Using this moment, Rob (now fully dressed) tiptoes out of the bedroom into the living room. He walks between Leon and Charles and heads toward the door. He touches Leon's knee as he passes him and says, "I think I'm gon' take off, Leon." Leon nods then leans back into the couch as Rob finishes with an awkward wave and exits.

Charles goes over to sit next to Leon on the couch. He looks at Leon but Leon has his eyes closed. "Leon, listen," Charles begins. "I know you love me; I love you too. I'm sorry I got so mad; we can work through this. I know we can. I can forget about this whole Rob debacle like nothing ever happened."

Leon sighs and opens his eyes. He wipes away the tears threatening to fall. "This isn't even about that," he says, "Let me ask the question I asked when I first saw you at that door tonight. What are you doing here?"

"I thought you were in danger so I-"

"How can you *think* I was in danger?" Leon cuts in, "As you can see, I'm perfectly fine. Nothing untoward or malicious happened to me tonight until you got here. Why are you here?"

Charles sighs and concedes. "The alarm went off and it alerted me. I tried calling you but you wouldn't pick up so I thought something dangerous was happening to you again. Then I checked the cameras and saw that someone was trying to break in through the back door so I raced over here as fast as I could."

Leon laughs quietly and sighs. He looks at his husband with newfound disappointment. "So, you could be my white knight in shining armor, huh? Charles, Rob was the one who opened the back door to throw out some trash. He didn't realize the alarms would go off if he didn't disarm the system. So, no break in here. Just a crazy, control freak spying on me."

Charles crosses his arms. "I wasn't spying, I was just trying to keep you safe."

Leon stands and faces Charles. "No, Charles, you crossed a line. You invaded my privacy. Here's what. Thank you for the security system, but I'm kindly asking you to take it back. I don't want it. I want it gone out of my home immediately tomorrow."

"Leon, no-"

"No, you listen. I'm a grown-ass independent man. I'm not your dead boyfriend, I'm not your estranged son. You've got to deal with that shit on your own. I can't be around for it." He pauses then walks toward the bedroom, "I have something for you." He goes into the bedroom then returns with a thick manila folder.

"What's that?" Charles asks.

Leon takes a seat next to Charles and opens the envelope. "I got a lawyer," he says, "And I filed these some weeks ago. I was hoping that I didn't have to give them to you, especially so soon, and especially after we were getting so close again within the past few weeks. But I think our time together has run out."

"Are these divorce papers?" Charles asks unbelievingly, "Wait, when did you do that? I thought we were working on us. I thought-"

"You thought many things, my love," Leon says sadly.

Charles begins sobbing. "I thought you said the door was open, I've been working so hard. I thought you said the door was open."

Leon wraps his arm around CHARLES' shoulder as he sobs. "I did," he says. "But now that door is closed."

✲ ✲ ✲

The next morning, Leon's apartment is buzzing with activity. There is a big cardboard box on the coffee table in the center of the living room and several smaller boxes on the floor next to the table.

Fears, Fantasies & Freedom

Rob walks into the living room from the bedroom carrying another box. He sets the box next to the coffee table when a loud ping rings out from his pocket. Rob takes out his phone, scans it for a minute and then begins to pace. After going back and forth a few times, he types a message and sends it. He starts pacing again as Brett and Leon enter the living room from the kitchen carrying boxes.

"Hey, thanks for coming over and helping me take down these cameras," Leon says, "Especially you Rob, I'm sorry you got caught up in all my drama. I couldn't sleep in here with those things up."

"Man, it's all good," Rob assures, "I was already involved anyway."

Brett places the box on the floor next to the front door then stretches, his arms high above his head. "From what you told me, last night sounds like it was crazy," he says. "When you came over to sleep at my place last night, I came to check on you in the middle of the night and you were tossing and turning on the couch. You still getting those dreams?"

Leon nods. "Yup."

"What dreams?" Rob asks.

Leon takes a seat on the couch. "I've been having some weird ass dreams ever since the night of the attack," he explains. "It's like there are masked people trying to break in through the doors and windows. Every time I go to secure one door, they start making headway through one of the windows and by the time I go to secure the windows, they're breaking through the backdoor."

Rob's phone dings and he checks it, then immediately slides it back into his pocket. Brett glances at him and narrows his eyes.

"Eventually they break in and overwhelm me and I fight for my life," Leon continues, "I keep trying to rip their masks off to see who they are. But every time I manage to pull one of the masks off, I wake up."

"Damn that's some intense shit," Rob says. He absent-mindedly rubs a spot on his head.

"The craziest thing is… You know when you feel like you know somebody?" Leon asks ominously, "That's how I feel when I see their face for the split second before I wake up. I just can't put my finger on it."

"I think you should move out of here," Brett advises. "They violated your space and your body and now they're violating your mind. And I'm not even just talking about the intruder. There's some bad juju up in this bitch." He shivers dramatically at this.

Rob's phone rings and he gets up from the couch almost nervously. The phone falls as he fishes it out of his pocket and he quickly snatches it up. "I'm gonna go take this," he says, excusing himself. Brett is watching him intently.

With Rob out of earshot, Brett turns to Leon and inquires, "So… this Rob thing is real, huh? Now he's hanging out with us in the daytime?"

Leon chuckles. Brett was always ready to get the tea on new people and new situations. "I'm just seeing where it goes. I like him," he admits. "It's pretty promising that he came over to help today, especially after everything he witnessed last night between Charles and me. I thought it would scare him away, but it doesn't look so."

"Hmm…" Brett replies, seemingly deep in thought. "So, when next are you seeing Charles' bitch ass?"

"He's coming by today to pick up all this camera shit and I actually have another box in my room packed with some of his shit that I don't want taking up space in here anymore," Leon answers.

"And then you're done with him for good right?" Brett questions.

Leon nods. "I really wanted to keep the peace for the next few months until after the green card interview, just so he wouldn't sabotage it. But this shit is too crazy. I'll just keep my fingers crossed and go into that interview on a wing and a prayer."

Rob returns from taking his private call and Leon stands up to make a request of him, "Rob, can you help me move these boxes over to the door?" Leon gestures at the boxes surrounding the coffee table.

"Sure, where do you want them?" Rob sets his phone down on the coffee table and begins picking up boxes. When they are done moving the boxes to the door, Leon asks Rob for another favor.

"And just one more favor, Rob. Help me with the last box in my room. That motherfucker's heavy." Rob nods and both men disappear into the bedroom to grab the last item.

Brett sits alone on the couch. Suddenly he perks up as Rob's phone vibrates on the coffee table. He glances towards the phone as it vibrates again. Brett thinks about the ethics of invading someone else's privacy. "Ugh, I shouldn't" he says to himself. But there was something that was a little off about Rob today and maybe this is just the Universe providing him an answer to his suspicions. He wasn't sure what he was suspicious about, but he needed to be sure if he was right to be suspicious. The phone vibrates one more time. "Maybe just a peek."

He picks up the phone and starts reading to himself. "'Are you over there right now?' 'I told you to stay away from him?' That's strange. Who is 'The Big Man?'"

Immediately Rob and Leon enter the living room balancing a big cardboard box between them. This startles Brett who drops Rob's phone. Leon and Rob lower the box to the ground and Rob runs to grab his phone from the ground.

"The fuck is you doin'?" Rob demands. Brett doesn't respond.

"Wait a minute, what's going on?" Leon asks, looking at Brett for an explanation.

"Man, why you going through my phone?" Rob demands again.

Brett stares at Rob before speaking, "Who is 'The Big Man?' and why is he so concerned about you being over here?"

Leon is confused, "Ok, seriously what's going on?"

Rob slips his phone into his pocket, "Yo, I'mma have to head out. Leon, do all your friends invade people's privacy like this?"

Brett stands up to face Rob, blocking his path. "Nuh-uh. You're not going anywhere before you explain some shit. I don't know what you're up to but those messages seemed suspect as hell. Leon, ask him to read what I just saw."

Leon appears to not be totally sold on what Brett was suggesting, "Brett, I don't want to-"

"Listen, somebody that he's got saved as 'The Big Man' is way too concerned about what he's got going on with you Leon," Brett insists, "I don't like the look of what I saw. 'I told you to stay away from him,' what the fuck does that mean?"

"You weren't supposed to be going through my shit, you don't know me like that," Rob counters.

"Actually, I don't know you at all. That's the problem," Brett shoots back.

Leon steps between then, deciding he must let cooler heads prevail. Nevertheless, Brett must have some reason for raising these questions about Rob and truthfully, Leon wanted to get to the bottom of any unanswered questions before moving forward. "Rob, I'm sorry but you just saw the shit I've been through with distrust and dishonesty in a relationship so if you can't explain what the hell is going on here, then I don't know how I feel about all this. Brett is my closest friend and I trust him a hundred percent. So, spill."

Rob backs away, "Man, I ain't got shit to say, I just gotta get out of here before…" He is interrupted by the ring of the doorbell.

"That must be Charles' bitch-ass," Brett grumbles.

Leon steps from between Brett and Rob and goes to answer the door. Standing in the doorway is Charles. Without a greeting, Leon gestures to the pile of boxes on the floor and says, "Your stuff is all there."

"Can we just talk a little before…" Charles begins. As he steps in, he spots Rob and Brett in the living room. "Oh, you have company."

"I'm just leaving," Rob says moving towards the entrance.

"Oh, like last night?" Charles asks.

"Charles, back off okay," scolds Leon. "You don't get the right to say shit to anybody after what you pulled. Rob has been there for me in ways that you can never even-"

Charles interjects incredulously, "*He's* been there for you! HAHA! That's rich. That is rich. You don't know this low-life."

"Man, I'm not gonna keep putting up with you talking down to me!" Rob says, visibly upset, "I'm getting real tired of this shit. I'm just trying to get out of here." He motions to leave, but Brett once again blocks his path.

"Wait a fuckin' minute. Hold up, hold up. You're getting real tired of what? As I understand you only met this man last night?" Brett inquires.

"Yo, get out of my way and don't ask me shit."

"Or what?" challenges Brett.

Both men face off. Brett suddenly pushes Rob who falls to the ground. His phone falls from his hand and slides across the floor. Brett dives for the phone, grabs it and selects something on the screen. Rob charges after him, "Gimme my shit!" he commands. All of a sudden Charles' phone starts ringing and everyone turns to look at him. There is silence for a beat.

"You want to answer that?" Brett asks, still holding Rob's phone.

Charles is dumbfounded. "I- Um-"

Brett speaks up. "Rob, you want to explain why you got Charles saved in your phone as 'The Big Man?'" Rob doesn't answer. Silence permeates the room.

Leon bursts into tears, "Y'all I can't do this."

Rob rushes to Leon's side. "I'm sorry Leon, I'm so sorry. I was going to tell you but I didn't know how to bring it up. I was just supposed to be a job, I didn't know that I'd fall for you like this."

"Fall for him?" Charles questions in disbelief, "I didn't pay you for that."

Leon pushes Rob away from him. "I need answers now! You two know each other!? You really hired a motherfucker to spy on me Charles? And Rob, I thought you were genuinely trying to get to know me these past few months! I can't fucking believe you're in his pocket."

Fears, Fantasies & Freedom

"It's not like that," Rob insists, "I was only supposed to keep your attention while y'all were separated so you didn't go out and find somebody else. But then shit got so complicated. I actually fell for you after all the time we've been communicating. I realized what I was doing fucked up. And when I tried to end it, he offered me twenty grand to stage the break-in and I really needed the money so I did it.

"I was only gonna scare you a little bit and then I'd be done, but then everything just went to shit. I fucked up. I fucked up real bad Leon and all I want is a chance."

Brett moves to console his best friend. He shakes his head as he wraps his arm around Leon's shoulders, "You can't trust a soul."

"Wow... I am speechless right now," says Leon, "Charles, you are more demented and deranged than I ever thought. I don't even want to argue, I don't even want an explanation. Take your shit and get out. I never want to see you again. Rob, it's obvious that I just need some time to myself. Trying to get into anything new was a mistake. I'm just ready to be done with all this. Just get out."

"Babe it wasn't even like that," Charles pleads, "I just wanted you to see how unsafe the neighborhood was. He wasn't supposed to actually hurt you."

"Don't call me babe," scoffs Leon "I'm nothing to you. You're nothing to me."

Fears, Fantasies & Freedom

"Leon, he's right. I never meant to hurt you," Rob joins in, "You weren't supposed to get hurt at all. He didn't even know we were seeing each other till last night when he showed up here. I was serious when I said I really fell for you. If you could just gimme a chance. Please."

Brett throws Rob's phone on the couch, "You really can't trust a motherfucker, can you?" Leon points to Brett and Rob and gestures towards the front door, "I thought I asked a motherfucker to get stepping?" Both men look at each other then back to Leon. Leon keeps pointing at the door, "Motherfuckers, get to stepping."

Defeat and dejection wash over their faces as Charles picks up some boxes and leaves through the front door. Brett picks up his phone off the couch and follows. Leon and Brett fall on the couch, feeling exhausted. They embrace for a moment then look at each other and shake their heads. Brett sighs then stands up. "Honey, we need to find you a new home. Come on, get your shoes on." The best friends stand and Leon grabs his shoes and quickly puts them on. They head towards the front door and exit. A soft click is heard as Leon shuts the door behind him.

6

The Caribbean Tree

The flags of a dozen countries waved ever so delicately in the gentle autumn breeze. The reds, golds and blues of the banners among the leaves created a kaleidoscopic show that I imagined sparked envy from the other trees and seating areas on the Yard. As a Jamaican, this one little spot was my home away from home while at school. It was the only place on campus one could go and hear multiple different non-American accents commingling and coalescing into a sonic tapestry of inter-island art.

That day I had just come from class and stopped to get a smoothie from the campus coffee shop. I'd already decided that I would lounge under the tree for about an hour then maybe I would head home. The four benches situated around the tree all had occupants. I spotted a free space next to my friend Brahman and headed over to sit next to him.

"What's up, Bram? I greeted him as we fist-bumped.

"Nothing much, you know," he replied, "just chilling out till my next class start."

Fears, Fantasies & Freedom

Next to him sat a Jamaican dude I was hardly acquainted with. Light-skinned and a douche face. I had never spoken to him before, but I reckon I probably had given him a head nod once or twice in passing. Today we ignored each other.

"Still nuh get my hire letter, you know?" I said to Brahman as I lowered my bag to the ground.

Brahman pushed a couple dreadlocks behind his ear and responded, "Dawg, me neither. I'm just gonna start looking at other options seriously, cause they're playing around now."

"I'm looking into other offers myself," I replied, adjusting the rainbow-colored band on my hand which had gotten stuck under my watch. "Just gonna cut my losses."

"Bram, come look here!" shouted a voice from the bench across from us. It was Tajil. He was good friends with light-skinned, douche-faced guy. The only difference was I was actually friendly with him. Brahman stood up to see what Tajil was talking about.

"Soon come," he said to me as he went over to the other bench.

I pulled out my phone and started scrolling Twitter as I sucked down my smoothie, dangerously flirting with crippling brain freeze. After a minute or so, Douche Face gets up and goes over next to Tajil and Brahman.

"Dawg, why you leave me over there with him?" I heard him say.

"What you talking 'bout?" Brahman asked him, lowering his voice.

At this point I was fully eavesdropping on the conversation but I pretended to still be all up on my Twitter timeline.

"You left me over there with the fag," Douche Face said.

"Yo, you're loud," Tajil chided.

"I don't give a fuck, he's a fag."

"He's cool," I heard Brahman say.

"Fire pan batty boy. I don't mingle with fags."

"And I don't mingle with assholes," I said, looking up.

At this point, all the guys were looking over at me. Brahman had a wry smile teasing the corners of his mouth and Tajil had his eyebrows raised so high, I was worried they wouldn't come down again.

"Dawg, fuck off and don't even talk to me," Douche Face retorted.

"What? Were you scared? Did you think I was gonna jump on you under the tree in front of everybody?" I asked, globules of faux concern dripping from my lips.

"Batty boy, watch yourself," he sneered.

"I'd watch myself if I were you honey, because your sexuality is so fragile you thought you'd catch the gay if you sat by me for even a minute," I countered, "You might want to check yourself."

He didn't respond. I smiled. I then reached into my pocket and fished out my earphones, plugged them into my phone and into my ears. I leaned back in my seat and stared up at the flags waving above me. Home. It felt just like home.

Fears, Fantasies & Freedom

7

That Used to Be His Beach

The sun's breath settled into my skin and I rejoiced in its warmth with a slow, steady sigh. I was laying on my stomach in ultimate relaxation mode when I heard a soft pop and felt some tension immediately release due to my Byron rubbing SPF 40 all over my back and shoulders while simultaneously working out the kinks in my joints. Maybe it was the massage that made me moan and not the sun at all, or maybe it was both. Honestly, it was probably the fact that his body pressed against mine and I could feel so many parts of him along my backside.

I turned my head to the side as he worked his fingers down to my bikini line. Through my sunglasses, I could see the sun glinting off his bald head and his sandy-brown face set with determination. As his hands worked my lower back, I took the moment to ogle his arms. They were like carved California redwoods, from his shoulder right down to his wrist. That's what attracted me to him in the first place. That and his mind. He was a thinker - he had lots of opinions and there was an almost poetic quality in the way he expressed them. I thought he was deep, something I was not. Which was fine, because I'm pretty, and that matters a lot at the end of the day.

"Charity, the way the lotion disappears into your dark skin as I rub it in is so marvelous. Your skin appears even richer and more supple afterwards and I just think it's a perfect metaphor for the struggle," he said, leaning into my ear.

"How so?" I asked.

"Well, for eons the black man has had his identity and culture covered, hidden or rubbed out by white society," he began. "But as I see the white lotion disappear into your black skin it just brings to mind the fight that our people of color have gone through and still, we persevere and come out on the other side even stronger, more resilient and bolder in our quest to shine."

"Oh…" I offered. See? Deep. Half the time I didn't know what he was talking about, but it tingled something inside me when he talked like that.

"Come on lovebirds! Y'all ain't gon' come in the water?" came a shout from behind us.

It was Renée, one of Byron's friends. Actually, everyone here was Byron's friend. I'd only met most of them within the last three weeks. I tapped Byron on his thigh and he got up off my back and lounged in the sand beside me. I flipped over and sat up to see Renée, Lindon and Kingston running out of the water to meet us on the sand.

Renée was nice enough, personality-wise. She was short with elfish ears and a nose like a button. I wouldn't call her pretty. Lindon was Byron's best friend; he was actually pretty hot. His body was pretty much sculpted by the gods themselves and his smile was like illicit drugs and sex rolled into one: white, dangerous, yet alluringly appealing. I'd only met Kingston that day, but everyone seemed to love him. He had an extroverted and sociable personality and I could tell he was intelligent. He was also decidedly handsome but had the beginnings of a receding hairline. I always pitied men in their twenties with hairline problems.

"Yes By! You are serving Nubian king, eighties model, construction worker realness with those arms and those swim trunks," Kingston said, dropping on the sand next to Byron. Byron smiled and seemed to blush a little, he rocked to the side and gave Kingston a little friendly nudge with his shoulder.

"Yo, I thought we came to the beach to swim and y'all two are just up here rubbing up on each other in the sand." Lindon said, squatting in front of us. I caught myself stealing repeated glances at the outline nestled between his open legs. Renée came up behind him and threw her arms around his neck, eventually resting her head in the nook between his shoulder and head.

"I'm just not in the mood for the water today," Byron said, stretching his arms then resting his head on my shoulder.

"You don't like water?" Kingston asked incredulously. I couldn't tell if he was being serious or facetious.

"Now, come on Kingston," Renée said impishly, "*You* know By loves to swim. You know everything about him, he's your man after all." She said 'man' while pantomiming quote signs with her fingers, making me a little uneasy. She glanced quickly in my direction then back at Kingston and offered slyly, "Well, he used to be."

I glanced at Kingston and he looked like a little boy just caught sneaking a cookie from the pantry in the middle of the night. He was obviously trying to avoid my eyes and he seemed particularly interested in the sand beneath his feet. Lindon let out a nervous chuckle and slowly stood up, shrugging Renée's arms from around his neck. He snickered nervously again then turned and skedaddled back toward the water.

I leaned over to Byron and whispered, "Is there something you need to tell me?" I tried to keep my face as pleasant as possible, as if someone had just crowned me Miss Universe, but I could tell my face was betraying me. I was feeling what Miss Colombia probably felt like after Steve Harvey mistakenly crowned her instead of Miss Philippines then took back the crown on national TV. And my face probably showed it.

"He claimed me," Byron murmured, "It's stupid, don't worry about it. Just a silly joke between friends."

"*He* did what now?" Kingston intervened, looking directly at Byron.

"Nothing," Byron offered, sidling up to me and putting his hand around my waist.

"No, repeat that," Kingston prompted tartly, smiling enormously while blinking ten times a second.

"I said, you claimed me, which is the truth." Byron confessed.

"Is that so?" Kingston said standing up, with that unnatural sickly-sweet smile still smeared on his face. He turned to Renée (who, during this whole exchange sat there fascinated and unmoving) and said caustically, "As you pointed out, Renée, I *do* know By quite well, so I know he does love the *water*, but he seems to prefer the *sand* now and… that's fine." He glared at me as he finished his sentence. "Charity, is it? Girl, will you be joining us in the water?"

"I'll pass for now," I returned his smile, determined not to crack, "But I'm so glad to be here with you all."

Kingston touched himself on the chest, leaned his head to the side and said, "Aw." He walked over to me and reached down to give me an air kiss, "Well, that's sweet," he purred.

"Yeah," I said, "And you're my favorite person here." I returned the air kiss as I said this.

Kingston stood upright and gave me the widest smile he could muster, "That's *so* cute," he replied, clearly unimpressed. His body blocked the direct rays of the sun, casting a long shadow over Byron and myself as he looked down on us where we sat.

"Enjoy the sand Byron, you know where I am if you want to get wet!" he called as he turned and skipped off toward the water with Renée close behind him. As I watched him dive into the sea, I decided that he was my least favorite person here and I could tell that I was his too.

8

Power and Purity

The blast of ice hit him squarely in the chest. He gasped as air escaped his lungs; his breath frostily visible in the moonlight. Tendrils of ice crept rapidly across his chest, eventually encapsulating his entire breastplate. The pressure was immense and the cold biting but Vanko knew that it could have been much worse had it not been for the enchanted armor the sprites had fashioned. He was knocked to the ground when the pixie's blast connected and he did not have the wherewithal to get back up. He stared up at the towering obelisk illuminated by the full moon in the backdrop.

He wondered what Osmund Ragal, the first Prime Councilmember of the Arlean Archipelago and the subject of the monumental obelisk, would think about the war. He probably wouldn't care much for it, Vanko thought, his goal was always unification, never dissension.

The grass on the grounds tickled the back of his neck and his pointed ears as the bangs and blasts of war raged around him. Slowly catching his breath, Vanko sat up and studied his surroundings.

He spotted a squadron of pixies clad in crimson Altivist uniforms bearing down on a group of goblins from the Resistance. They fought next to the Mirrored Pool in the center of Monument's Row. The pixies seemed relentless in their attack; launching blasts of elemental magic at the goblins who, to their credit, were fiercely defending and parrying the attacks with speed and dexterity.

One goblin leaped into the air and delivered what seemed to be a bone crushing punch to the face of one pixie as another launched a ball of fire at the punching goblin sending him flying into the pool.

Vanko averted his eyes and looked once again to the top of Ragal's Monument, where sprites and imps were engaged in heated battle. The imps from the Resistance launched curse after curse at the sprites who kept blocking the attacks with protection charms, only pausing to throw out offensive spells of their own. As both airborne parties flitted around the sharp point of the obelisk, Vanko watched as a jet of light launched from the hand of a sprite connected with the forehead of an imp as he glided around the monument dodging another attack.

Fears, Fantasies & Freedom

The imp's shriek pierced through the already loud cacophony of the battle and his body went limp as it hurtled towards the ground. Just before the imp crashed onto the pavement, Vanko reached out with his mind and caught the imp, slowly resting his unconscious body on the pavement.

Vanko looked around to see if anyone had noticed, but the rest of the elves were still engaged in battle with the faction of pixie defectors who were fighting on the side of the Resistance. He wasn't quite sure why he had saved the imp; Vanko was an Altivist after all and the imp was a member of the Resistance. He knew he had started questioning his part in the war and in the Altryte administration all together, but his protection of a Resistance member was borderline treason, and he wasn't sure he was okay with it. But then, he wasn't even sure what he was okay with anymore, he had thought during the campaign before the election that he was doing the right thing, now he couldn't say that with much conviction.

One could argue that the beginnings of the war can be traced back to the campaign season of the last election. The Arlean Archipelago was at the tail-end of the Orgen administration, which many say was one of the most progressive decades in Arlea.

It was the first Premier Council in the history of the republic to have two goblins among the eleven-member body and the first to have an imp, Karab Orgen, as the Prime Councilmember. The Council had representatives from seven of the eight islands that made up the archipelago; the most in the history of the government. Orgen improved faerie-giant relations by being the first Prime Councilmember to visit Senthy, the island of the giants, in over 80 years.

Orgen's administration was also instrumental in forging and maintaining strong bonds with the governments of the two merpeople city states located under the seas surrounding the archipelago. Relations between faeries themselves seemed to be the most positive it had been in years as all five faerie races appeared to get along quite well. More sprites and pixies seemed to understand their privilege and openly regretted years of oppression by their kind towards goblins and imps. Though this period of governance was widely praised for its progress it was still criticized by many for its apparent failures.

Fears, Fantasies & Freedom

Some critics who supported the opposition believed that the Orgen administration had stripped away the religious traditions and mores that the republic was founded on. They believed that the power of the Pantheon (the three deities said to have created everything) was downplayed in the Orgen administration and that the decision to remove the Call to Pantheon as the opening to Congress gatherings was a fatal error on the part of the Council. Orgen and his administration argued that many faeries no longer worshipped the Pantheon and therefore to be inclusive, it was prudent to remove the archaic practice from Congress gatherings. The opposition Congress members never forgave Orgen and the Premier Council for what they claimed was blasphemy of the highest order and made it the cornerstone issue of their opposition to Orgen.

Orgen and the Premier Council were criticized by supporters for not legalizing procreation between the faerie races. Orgen thought that this was too radical a cause and refused to even consider it; this, some of his supporters argued, was his biggest failure. Opposition Congress members and their supporters however, were in full agreement with this measure and it was possibly the only issue that they and Orgen aligned with.

Fears, Fantasies & Freedom

The opposition secretly hated the fact that sprites, pixies and elves were fraternizing and cohabiting with goblins and imps, but that idea of inequality had gone out of fashion over the years and no one would openly admit to their prejudice. The fact that an imp was the Prime Councilmember was already terrible enough; they could not bear to imagine a republic where legalized interrace procreation was a reality.

Vanko was a member of the opposition members of Congress. At 38, he was one of the youngest lawmakers in the archipelago. He was quite religious but having been adopted by rich, imp parents as an infant, he did not share many of the racial prejudices that his colleagues in Congress ascribed to.

Vanko grew up in Cerean Center, the biggest city in Arlea and the capital of the island Ceris. The Cerean Center was the financial epicenter of the nation and had always been the most racially heterogeneous city in the archipelago, so Vanko grew up with friends from all five races.

Fears, Fantasies & Freedom

After completion of his secondary education, Vanko left Ceris and moved to the island of Myro. He decided to attend the Myro Academy in Ragalton to pursue a career in politics. Ragalton was the national capital and the center of politics and policy in Arlea. While in college, Vanko mostly associated with other elves as well as sprites and pixies. One of the sprites he got close with was Sheena Altryte. She came from an old Myran family with a rich political legacy. She wasn't a particularly brilliant student but she was immensely popular and possessed great charisma. Together they both climbed the ranks of the political system quite quickly after graduation, with both earning seats in Congress by their thirties.

They were a part of the fierce Opposition during both Orgen administrations and as the election cycle loomed, Altryte appeared as the frontrunner to lead the Opposition in what would be a tough battle to secure an election win.

Sheena Altryte's opposition party became known as the Altivists and they approached the election campaign in a bizarre and unprecedented way. First, Altryte's Premier Council nominees included no goblins and no imps. It was an eleven-member strong conglomeration of pink sprites, blue pixies and green elves. Vanko didn't think much of it and he never questioned it, especially because he was one of the elves selected to serve on Altryte's potential Premier Council. Altryte justified this by saying that her Council picks were not selected based on prejudice but by performance.

The Altivists adopted the motto "Path to Power and Purity." They ran on a campaign of bringing back the Pantheon to prominence and preserving the purity of the faerie races. Many of the sprites, who had for centuries been at the top of the social and political hierarchy in the archipelago, ate up the Altivist message like hot honey loaves.

The prominence of goblins and imps in the economic and political systems of Arlea had some sprites, pixies and elves feeling less than. As equality progressed, it became more unpopular to oppose it, but the Altivists had done what no politician had dared do in the last thirty years and spoke openly about returning sprites, pixies and elves to distinction. They employed ideas that had long become forgotten into their political rhetoric.

Fears, Fantasies & Freedom

    Altryte posited that the Pantheon intended sprites, pixies and elves to be the natural leaders of the archipelago and that is why they were given stronger abilities unique to each race. Sprites had the ability to cast enchantments and charms, pixies had the ability to wield the elements to their liking and elves were naturally gifted with psionic abilities. According to Altivists these were the abilities that shaped the modern republic and what separated them from goblins and imps whose abilities were seen as either inessential or destructive. Goblins possessed unparalleled strength, speed and agility while imps had the ability to cast curses, jinxes and hexes. Vanko never quite understood why those abilities were not honored like the ones of sprites or elves, but he had become content in believing that the Pantheon had created his race superior to others.

    Political pundits and analysts predicted a crushing defeat for the Altivists in the election. Their reasoning was that the citizens of Arlea were committed to progress and therefore would never want to return to the days of goblin servitude and imp banishment.

Little did they know how wrong they were; Altryte's popularity rapidly grew and she eventually gained a large following of sprites, pixies and elves who had apparently longed to return to the world of their great-grandparents. Analysts approximated that more than 90 percent of sprites, a little over 70 percent of pixies and just under half of the elfin population were pro-Altivists.

Vanko was excited at the time about the prospect of winning the election and becoming a part of the Premier Council but the relationship with his parents had suffered drastically as the campaign went on. By the time only a few weeks remained before the election, Vanko had been estranged from his parents for more than four months.

Vanko sighed as he remembered his parents, who by now hadn't spoken to him in more than two years. The ice on his chest had now dissipated and he rose to his feet to rejoin the battle. Vanko had never been in a war before, but he had rigorous combative training like all politicians did. Arleans believe that if you want to lead the nation you should also be able to defend it, so political training also included rigorous offensive and defensive magical courses. Despite this, Vanko was not prepared to see the forest of bodies strewn across Monument's Row.

Fears, Fantasies & Freedom

As he ran into battle, he almost tripped over a body wearing the Altivists' signature red uniform. It was an elf like him, his pistachio skin shimmered in the moonlight, as the lunar rays reflected off the water droplets sticking to him. His entire body was wet; he was probably drowned by a water-wielding pixie. Vanko dismissed the fallen soldier and hurried over to where his squadron of elves were still engaged in fearsome combat with the defector Resistance pixies.

"Great of you to show up again Vanko!" yelled one elf, while dodging a well-aimed shard of ice from a pixie. This was Ringo, an elf Vanko had only recently met since the beginning of the war.

"I got hit!" Vanko yelled back, "I was down for a while."

"Well shut up and start fighting!" Ringo replied, "We need everybody right now, these fucking pixies are strong."

Vanko felt a robust gust of wind rush pass him and watched as it lifted Ringo off his feet, knocking him to the ground. Ringo remained motionless lying on the earth. Vanko looked for the source of the wind and spotted the pixie, clad in her black Resistance uniform. Her eyes were fire and she held a menacing grin as she turned to look at Vanko, "Your turn," she said. She raised her hands and summoned a squall that hurled Vanko several yards away.

Vanko groaned as he struggled to his feet, the pixie was already running towards him, readying for another attack. Vanko flicked his head in her direction and flung her back in the air. She called the wind for help and floated to her feet instead of crashing to the ground like Vanko had intended. He used his telekinesis to levitate above her, hoping to intimidate her.

From his vantage point he could see different fights like the one he was engaging in, taking place across Monument's Row. Goblins versus sprites across the Mirrored Pool, elves versus elves on the steps of Lynden Memorial, imps versus pixies and elves on the *roof* of Lynden Memorial - any combination of combat one could think of.

The pixie he was fighting seemed to be inhaling deeply, readying for another attack.

"Oh shit!" he yelled, he knew what was coming. She immediately exhaled in his direction blowing his airborne body up and away into the sky. As he careened through the air, Vanko took a second to acknowledge how refreshing the cool, night air felt on his face. He wondered why he couldn't have been playing with the wind-wielding pixie like he used to as a child instead of fighting one.

Fears, Fantasies & Freedom

He regretted the violent and contentious life that adulthood had placed on him. Sure, he still had many pixie colleagues, after all most of them were Altivists. But those pixies along with a great chunk of elves that fought for the Resistance made him question his role in the government and his role in the war.

Vanko's wandering mind was jolted back to reality when he suddenly realized he was in freefall, rapidly tumbling toward the ground like the imp he had saved earlier. He closed his eyes and tried to focus, willing his telekinesis to slow his descent and wield back control of his body. The sensation of using one's telekinesis on oneself remained an intensely queer feeling, no matter how many times tele-elves do it. Even levitating produced the same sensation which is why most elves seldom do, leaving airborne antics to the winged sprites and flying-capable imps. The Pantheon probably intended it that way, anyway.

Vanko finally reclaimed concentration and floated of his own accord back to where the pixie he was fighting was standing.

"You don't give up do you, Altryte scum?" she sneered as he drifted down in front of her.

"Actually, I ne-" Vanko's retort stopped suddenly as his voice caught in his throat.

"Were you saying something?" the pixie asked, cocking her head to the side, feigning concern. Vanko felt the air rushing out of his lungs, stifling him. He fell to the ground and clutched at his neck, gasping for air. The pixie took a few steps over to him as he lay on the floor clawing at the grass, at his throat, anywhere, for an ounce of air. She stood over him, twirling her index finger in a circular motion, as if siphoning the air from his lungs and spooling it into thread around her finger. He needed that thread!

"I… can't… breathe," he gasped.

"Now where have I heard that before?" the pixie questioned, squatting in front of him, still twirling her finger.

Vanko knew death was coming, he could feel it. Feel *him*. The deity of death must've had a busy night that night considering all the lives that were lost. Vanko knew the deity's next appointment was with him. His eyes slowly went dark as he felt Death's pallid lips against his. As his lungs emptied, he relinquished his form into Death's icy embrace. It was always a known fact that Death was the first deity any faerie would meet, it was only through Him that one could meet the rest of the Pantheon. As the final vestiges of sight vanished, Vanko's last image would be the acerbic smile on the periwinkle face of the defector pixie.

"No peace without justice, Alty" she whispered, as he descended into darkness.

As he lost consciousness, Vanko was transported back to the day of the election. All the faeries were gathered in the city halls, town halls or village squares to hear the results. Vanko himself was with Altryte and the other members of the Opposition's prospective Premier Council in front of the congressional building in Ragalton. It was an intensely close election and they were all shuddering in nervous excitement.

The Altivists had won enough votes so far to secure three of the eight islands. Redland, the Foam Isles and Latherwood had gone to the Altivists; while Ceris, Landoffer and Dax went to the Progressors; the Orgen administration's expectant successors. One island, Senthy, went to the Uniters, another group in the running for the Premier Council. Senthy was a particularly curious island as only a small faerie community resided there and they were descendants of families who lived in harmony with the giant population who dominated the island.

Fears, Fantasies & Freedom

As the night went on, the citizens of Arlea waited with bated breath to see what the outcome of the election would be. This was shaping up to be one of the most historic election results in the history of the archipelago. This was an election that would either pave the way for the future or launch the archipelago eons back into the past. The last island to be counted was Myro. Vanko knew that it would be particularly hard for the Altivists to take Myro. Most of the citizens in the main city, Ragalton were Progressors and Ragalton held more than half of the island's population. The only way they could win in Myro was if the pro-Altivists in the interior of the island came out in droves to vote that day.

The Elector-General, Lyle, soon came on the stage in front of the congressional building to announce the results. The rotund goblin carried a solitary envelope in his hand as he walked to the center of the stage. He wore a serious expression on his tawny face as he cleared his throat in preparation for his announcement.

Fears, Fantasies & Freedom

The crowd in front of the congressional building was truly massive and included people from all hues of the political spectrum. Lyle seemed to be overwhelmed for a quick second as he raised his eyes to look over the multitude. He cleared his throat once again and signaled the young sprite standing at the far left of the stage. The sprite motioned her hand toward him and the goblin seemed to shudder as an enchantment took hold of him.

"I have just received this unopened envelope from the hand of the head ballot counter," Lyle said. His voice boomed across the crowd, ringing as loud as a giant's cry. The sprite had used a *vozalta* charm on him, which exponentially magnified his voice.

"As with all other results, the ballots have been counted by the impartial and independent members of the Elector-General's council and have been safeguarded against charms, curses or any enchantments that might alter the veracity of the votes," Lyle continued.

"The voting for the island of Myro concluded at 16 hours this evening and the results are now in. Considering the outcome of the votes in the other islands, the Premier Council nominees that win Myro will lead the government at the beginning of next year and their chief council member will be the Prime Councilmember of the Arlean Archipelago. Without further ado, I will read the results."

Lyle opened the envelope and removed a rectangular piece of paper from within. The goblin's face deepened from its pale orange to a rusty color. He swallowed for a second before continuing.

"In a vote of 573,672 to 502,428, the Altivists have won the island of Myro and thus…" he paused to clear his throat, "… and thus they will make up the 54th government of the Arlean Archipelago."

The crowd erupted in simultaneous cheers and outrage. Sprites were flying in the air, zooming through the wind in celebration. Some fire-wielding pixies were shooting flames into the air in festivity; while goblins were seen quickly retreating in stark disappointment. A couple of imps cursed the ground, making wherever they stepped turn into a mucky pile of goo; an ancient sign of an imp wallowing in despair.

Sheena Altryte for her part spread her wings and flew into the sky. She made a big show of producing twinkling lights to trail her as she flew through the night sky; captivating the audience. She then came to a stop above the stage and methodically lowered herself until her feet were just mere inches away from the floor. She hovered there and waved her hands to signal the members of her Council to join her on the stage.

Fears, Fantasies & Freedom

She cast a sideways glance at Lyle, who took that as his sign to exit. Vanko and the other prospective council members made their way to the stage standing in a line with Altryte hovering in the middle.

"This," she said, "is progress." Her voice echoed across the spellbound crowd. She had also cast the *vozalta* charm.

"Praise the Pantheon. Let's return Arlea to glory. This is the path to power and purity!"

As the crowd cheered and the Progressor allies fled the scene in Vanko's mind, he was pulled back to the present as he suddenly felt the air rushing back into his lungs. He heaved and gasped as the rush of air fought to fill up his chest cavity. His vision slowly returned and he saw that the pixie he was fighting with was walking away, obviously to rob some other poor elf of his breath.

Vanko reached out with his mind and grabbed hold of her. He was still panting on the floor and too weak to move but he held on to her with his mind as she struggled against his telekinetic grip. He made sure to keep her back turned to him and to keep her hands immobile so she couldn't use any more wind attacks against him.

With a subtle twist of his head, he heard a loud crack emanate from the pixie and an agonizing scream leave her mouth. Her right arm was angled quite awkwardly and Vanko was sure he could see the bone in her upper arm pushing against her skin.

    He twisted his head again and the loud cracking noise returned, but this time Vanko could see blood dripping from the pixie's left arm and a bone protruding from her forearm. As Vanko regained his strength, he crawled over to where he held the pixie in his grip. He slowly raised her a few inches off the ground and rotated her body to face him. He was on all fours as he looked up at the broken pixie. He clutched at the grass between his fingers and observed her contorted face. He could tell she was a pretty pixie. She probably had all the attention of the boys or girls wherever she went. Her skin was a soft blue that darkened just around the eyes, looking almost purple, like an imp. Tears streamed down her face and pathetic whimpers escaped her twisted mouth.

    "Do you like seeing me on all fours, pixie?" Vanko asked. He had no idea why he said this. He supposed he wanted to channel the behavior of a true Altivist leader. The pixie did not answer.

    "You should," Vanko said, "That's how the goblins used to kneel before us back in the day. On all fours, like the worthless filth they are."

Fears, Fantasies & Freedom

Vanko's childhood friend Tommin suddenly flashed in his mind. Tommin was a neighbor who first taught him how to make flying dragons out of pieces of parchment. A practice Vanko still upheld when sitting in his office bored. He would fold and crease and refold pieces of parchment until it made the perfect dragon that could glide for more than five seconds in the air. He had really liked Tommin as a kid and didn't really think of him as worthless filth. But Altivist rhetoric had become a cornerstone in his life now and he had to uphold those values. He was sure the Pantheon must have created them as lesser beings. Lesser beings that one could love but would never be one's equal.

"You're a pixie," Vanko said, slowly bringing himself to his feet, "Why would you join the Resistance? Why would you ever fight for those dirty goblins and untrustworthy imps?"

As he stood, he stared into the pixie's eyes and shook his head. "What a waste. But it's for the better. The Altivists only need loyal pixies. Loyal sprites, loyal elves and loyal *fucking* pixies." At that, he motioned with his arm and the pixie's neck snapped. He released his grip and her limp body fell to the floor. Her eyes were still open, moonlight reflecting off their glossy surface.

Vanko could not contend with the thought that he was fighting for an unjust cause. He must be right. He had dedicated decades of his life to this brand of politics and there was no way he could ever fathom that he could be wrong. If he was wrong, then the Pantheon would not have caused the Altivists to win. The Pantheon was as sick and tired as he was of the blasphemy and disregard for the deities espoused by the Orgen administration and no number of protests or marches would change that. For Vanko, that was the most annoying part of the leadup to the war. The goddamn protests. Every major city in Arlea had protests.

When Altryte was inaugurated, the Progressor allies held a massive protest the next day in Ragalton. Faeries had come from all over the archipelago to march in defense of progress and equality. Vanko distinctly remembered when Orgen had discontinued the Call to Pantheon in congressional meetings; nobody had shown up to march then. But now faeries wanted to march for everything.

Fears, Fantasies & Freedom

When Altryte banned goblins and imps from within the perimeter of Ragalton, their pixie and elf sympathizers turned up to march. When Altryte outlawed cohabiting between different races, protests broke out in the Cerean Center, Xenia Bay in Landoffer, Fryar in Latherwood and of course, Ragalton. The protests became increasingly violent as Altryte enacted new discriminatory laws and introduced rollbacks to legislation that had specifically protected goblins and imps. According to the Altryte administration, if they wanted equality so bad, then they didn't need *special* protections.

Vanko walked away from the pixie's lifeless body and made his way toward the Mirrored Pool where goblins and sprites were still waging war. He wanted his chance at taking out a goblin too. He felt a slight tremor as he ran towards the pool. He jumped over dead faeries and dodged spells and elements on his way to the sprites. As he approached them, the ground shook a little again, only this time with more force.

As he approached the sprites and readied to join the fray, he glimpsed out of the corner of his eye a goblin leaping towards him. Before he could duck, a punch connected with his jaw, he heard a loud crack and knew his jaw bone was broken.

Vanko doubled over in pain, spitting out blood and a couple teeth onto the ground. The goblin followed that up with a roundhouse kick in Vanko's abdomen sending him flying into the pool. As he landed in the water, Vanko swore he felt another tremor, but this one was even more intense than the last. And this time he knew it was not his imagination.

Water and duck excrement filled his mouth as he sank to the bottom of the pool. He opened his eyes but could see nothing in the murky water, he only felt the ground shake once more. Vanko tried desperately to swim to the surface, but he was weak from the pain the goblin's blows had caused. He let his body go lifeless and willed himself to float to the surface of the water. As he floated to the top, Vanko assessed that he had at least two broken ribs to go with his broken jaw, there was no way he could actively continue to take part in the battle. He had to retreat. The ground shook again and Vanko noticed that the battlefield had gone silent.

Opening his eyes, he turned his head while floating on the water to see what was happening in Monument's Row. He looked toward Ragal's Monument and noticed figures as tall as the obelisk silhouetted against the night sky. One of them had his hand wrapped around the center of the obelisk. Vanko closed his eyes and let out a weak sigh. The giants had not interfered in faerie matters for hundreds of years.

Fears, Fantasies & Freedom

Why would they start now? All the Altivists were trying to do was make Arlea great again. The giants had no dog in this fight. Vanko coughed weakly and wondered whose side the giants were fighting on, because the tide of the war had just changed. Giants were impervious to magic and faeries' diminutive stature posed no threat to their immense figure. Vanko watched as the giant holding on to Ragal's Monument tore the obelisk from the ground like a pesky blade of grass and held the structure high in the air. His massive arm eclipsed the moonlight and he threw his head back and bellowed.

"No justice! No peace!"

Vanko got his answer, and he closed his eyes and sank back to the depths of the pool. The murky water enveloped him and filled his orifices. As his body touched the bottom of the pool, he welcomed the embrace of the deity's frosty grip.

9

Coming Out on the Other Side

Mathieu

I am scared. Not that anyone would know. I've perfected my happy façade for years now and it's since become second nature. I push open the glass doors of Smultor Inc. and paint a contented smile on my visage as I wave to the receptionist.

"Hey, how was the weekend?" she asks as I scan my company ID badge.

I let out an exaggerated sigh, "Just thankful for the rest I got," I reply, "Can't believe it's Monday already."

She pushes back two long braids behind her left ear and says something that I pretend to hear. I chuckle politely and respond, "I know right!" then quickly shuffle off to the elevator. I get off at the sixth floor and head over to my cubicle. I drop my bag on the desk and power on the computer.

"Hey Mathieu, how was the weekend?" I hear behind me. I turn and see Jozlyn, who had rolled her chair over to my workstation from the other side of the room. She is wearing a bright marigold blouse tucked neatly into a scarlet pencil skirt. I notice her hands resting on the arms of the chair; she seems to have gotten a manicure over the weekend as she was sporting bright yellow nails.

"It was fine," I reply, "Just thankful for the rest, can't believe it's Monday already." I finish with a smile and an exaggerated sigh.

"Right?" she responds quickly. I can already tell that she is gearing up to tell me all about her weekend. I bet it was filled with magic. "You have no idea what I did!" she says.

I do. It was all over Instagram. "Omigod! Yeah! You went to Atlantic City!" I say this about two octaves higher than I usually would.

"It was everything!" she says, "I won so much fucking magic, you have no idea."

"I bet you did," I smile, "New hair, I see." I point to the wavy, blonde tresses cascading around her caramel face. She giggles a little and gently throws her head back, exposing the little mole just by her right eye.

"Cost me a fortune, about 2800 cantas for the weave alone and another 600 to have my girl, Rica put it in."

"You spent *all* that magic on hair?" I ask incredulously.

Fears, Fantasies & Freedom

Prring! I spin in my chair to see I have a new email from my cousin Tevin. Subject line: DEM SEND ME BACK. Jozlyn says something but I ignore her with a chuckle and nod. I click open Tevin's email to see what he said.

Cuz, I'm back in Bahamas. Uncle Sam send me back. I hear somebody rat me out. I don't know who. But is last week they came and put me in handcuffs and everything. Anyway, I'm just letting you know what happen. Take care of yourself. And be careful, keep an eye out. I hear what Mr. Trump say. They cracking down Mathieu, try sort out yourself and get your papers together.

Also, I don't have that much magic. See if you can send a little magic my way, please. Sharelle needs school supplies and all the magic I made in America not available to me right now. I don't need much, 200 cantas should be enough.

Alright cuz, take care.

Dammit, I think. I glance to see if Jozlyn is still behind me, but thankfully she takes the hint and has already rolled back over to her workstation. I slowly close my eyes and allow my head to fall into my hand. I rub my eyes and pinch the bridge of my nose as I try to fully grasp what had happened to my cousin. I'm now more scared for myself than I was this morning. With a heavy sigh, I raise my head and click open the web browser on the computer. The homepage is filled with the latest news:

Fears, Fantasies & Freedom

SIX KILLED IN CLASH BETWEEN WHITE SUPREMACISTS AND PROTESTERS IN HUNTSVILLE, ALABAMA.

TRUMP EXPANDS IMMIGRATION BAN AND CLAMPS DOWN ON UNDOCUMENTED IMMIGRANTS.

RUMORS SWIRL ABOUT C.E.O.'S INVOLVEMENT AS PROBE INTO MAGIC HEIST AT CMB INVESTMENTS INTENSIFIES.

"Morning Mathieu, you okay?" a strong but troubled voice says. I look up into the amber eyes of Lancaster, my boss, looking over my cubicle partition. The regular sternness in his demeanor seems to be banished for the moment and instead, something resembling a hint of concern furrows his eyebrows a little. His chiseled jawline sports a subtle five o'clock shadow; minuscule hair dotting the rich caramel of his skin. His head is titled at a slight angle and his usually intense eyes seem to soften.

"I-I'm okay," I quickly stammer, "just reading the crazy news this morning." I let out a small scoff and flippantly wave at the computer.

"It's a mess out there I tell you," Lancaster replies, his once concerned voice regaining that baritone timbre I am used to. "How was your weekend?" He adjusts the brown leather strap of his work bag on his shoulder. He is wearing a tan suit today, with a dolphin shaped tie clip. I'm glad he chose the cyan shirt to complement the look.

"It was actually really great," I lie, "Glad to be back at work though, I love a Monday."

"You're the only person I'd ever hear saying that," Lancaster chuckles, "Don't forget to live while you're young." He nods and heads down the hallway to his corner office. He waves to another colleague behind me and throws a quick good morning through the supervisor's office door on his way down. As he gets to his glass office door, he flicks his hand and the door opens, his work bag slides off his shoulder and floats into the open office. Lancaster follows his bag in, and with another flick of his hand, the bag settles on his desk and the door closes behind him. He settles into his chair and rubs his eyes for a bit then motions to something out of my view. A moment later a cup of steaming coffee comes soaring across his office and lands itself on the table in front of him.

Fears, Fantasies & Freedom

I end my possible creepy surveillance of Lancaster and turn back to my computer. I wonder how it must feel to have so much magic that you use it liberally to do things like open doors and levitate objects daily. The last time I used my magic for anything more than a transaction was when I was putting together IKEA furniture three months ago, when I moved into my new apartment. I'm not strapped for magic, I'm just frugal. As an immigrant, I never know when I might need the extra magic if dire circumstances hit.

I type in CMB Investment's web address into the browser to access my account. I have 9,347 cantas worth of magic in my account. I can spare 200 for my cousin Tevin. I transfer the magic, then click open my email and type out a quick note to him.

Hey Tev,
Me send the magic, okay. 200. Sorry to hear they send you back. Thanks for the advice, I'll keep my eyes open. Never know when the same can happen to me. Tell everybody I say hi. Kiss Sherelle for me. OO

I close the window and open Photoshop. It's about time I start some actual work this morning.

I get home that evening a little after six. I spy two green eyes some feet away in the darkness looking in my direction as I open the door. I step in and close the door behind me as the green eyes move closer and closer to me. Soft fur rubs against my trouser leg and I smile and bend down to pick up the culprit.

"Hi Mr. Sweeney, are you hungry?" I coo. He whispers a soft purr into my ear and rubs his head into my stubble. I reach for the light switch along the wall and flip it. The ginger tabby looks up at me, his green eyes glistening.

"I missed you too boy," I plant a quick kiss on his forehead and shoo him onto the carpet. I drop my work bag at the door and kick off my shoes. I untuck the green plaid shirt and unbuckle my belt, never fully removing it. I walk through the living room and pick up the TV remote off the coffee table. I turn on the TV then throw the remote in the burgundy sofa and make my way to the kitchen. I open the fridge and grab a beer, twisting it open as I walk back to the sofa. I sit on one end and stretch my legs. Mr. Sweeney saunters into the living room as I take a swig of the beer. He jumps onto the sofa and settles at my feet. I take another swig and stretch to rest the bottle on the coffee table without disturbing Mr. Sweeney.

Fears, Fantasies & Freedom

The TV is on cable news. It is two talking heads and the pasty anchor who everyone liked. He is cute if you ask me; tall, a silver fox, a winner smile. Cute, but a little pasty. He could do with some sun. He is joined by that regular black political analyst with the hard face and bald head as well as that blonde 27-year-old 'expert' on magic management. Her face is pretty but holds a permanent condescending glare and know-it-all smile.

Black talking head is harping on about how government regulation of magic is corrupt and goes against the values of liberty and equality that the country was founded on. Blonde talking head keeps reiterating that it is only a *certain type* of people that would call for the deregulation of magic and those are the *same types* that steal magic from reserves on a regular basis.

I slowly pull my feet from under Mr. Sweeney's body, he barely peeks through his left eye at me then goes back to ignoring me. I take another mouthful of the beer from the table then pull open the small drawer in the table facing me. I remove a small, round, aluminum container from the drawer, along with a small bag of green herbs and a small, blue-stained, glass pipe. I open the baggie and take out a sizeable nub of the weed.

Fears, Fantasies & Freedom

I screw open the aluminum container to reveal interlocking prongs on the inside of both the cover and the base. I place the nub on the pronged side of the base then placed the cover on top to begin grinding the weed. When I'm done grinding, I open the grinder and take in a whiff of the strong aroma. I scoop out some of the contents and pack the bowl of the glass pipe compactly. I stare at the pipe then snap my fingers. That will probably cost me about 5 cantas, but what's the point of having magic if I can't use it to toke up. The weed lights up and I immediately take a nice, long hit of the pipe and hold the smoke in for a few seconds. Then let it out.

"There was a time when people used to have control of their magic. How can we really say we live in a free country if the government continues to regulate citizens' magic?" Black talking head shouts.

"There was also a time when only monarchs and nobility had magic and peasants were restricted from having access to it." Blondie shouts back, "You people should be grateful that you live in a country where you can pull yourself up by the bootstraps and amass as much magic you want."

"*You people? Grateful?* Are you *bleep*-ing kidding me?"

"Alright watch the language there Byron," the anchor scolds.

Fears, Fantasies & Freedom

I reach for the remote to change the channel. I take another hit of the pipe as I scroll the channel guide. I decide to watch some more cable news. I lean back into the sofa and relax as the effects of the weed are beginning to hit me.

I retrieve my wallet from my pocket and pull out my CMB canta card. The little display in the top right-hand corner tells me I have 9,141 cantas in my account. Oh right, I forgot about the new 1 canta tax on fire magic. I'll have to be more careful about using petty magic. I don't have Lancaster-type amount of magic. Lancaster...those amber eyes.

I sit up and fish out a purple lighter from the drawer; lighting the pipe to take another hit. I hear the news talking about the capture of some guy who was running a sex trafficking ring. His wife is on the program denying the claims and pleading with America to remember that suspects are deemed innocent until proven otherwise. A mess.

I begin to doze off on the sofa for a second before I see something weird out of the corner of my eye. I swear I see blue ripples around the edges of the living room wall. Not the edges of the wall, that is inaccurate. More like the edges of the room, or more accurately a disruption in the space. It's as if the air is coalescing then tearing apart. Then rinse and repeat. I can't necessarily *see* the air but I am seeing something. I would compare it to – *Ring!*

The sound of the ringing phone breaks me from cannabis-induced reverie. I get up to answer the phone and see that it's my friend Yosef calling.

"Yosef, what's up? I ask.

"Me alright you know? You hear about Tevin?" he asks.

"Him send me an email this morning, brother," I sigh, "What a travesty."

"Mathieu, I'm worried you know. What if – ?" Yosef begins.

"What if nothing Yosef. Calm down. I'll be fine." I try to assure him.

"You can't say that for sure, though, can you? Any day they can just come and knock on you door and *bam*, you gone."

I'm hyper focused on making coherent thoughts and saying actual things when I speak while high. At this moment, I do not have the patience to explain to Yosef why I know I'll be fine. I also can't bear to admit that I too am worried. I too am scared. I didn't want to get deported. This country may have its ills (and believe me it does) but this is where I have made my life. This is my opportunity to become successful and earn mountains of magic. I can't help that I am *illegal*; they've made it increasingly difficult for immigrants to gain citizenship in this country.

Fears, Fantasies & Freedom

Nobody is lining up to marry me, and I don't have enough magic yet to convince anyone to enter some arrangement with me. So, for now, I'm biding my time, till I can make it right. I say none of this to Yosef. Because deep down I know that he knows all of this.

"I'll be fine, Yosef, don't worry. Good night, k?"

"Alright bro, tomorrow," he says, then I hang up the phone. It's time I went to bed too.

The next morning as I enter the office and sit down, Jozlyn slides over to my desk.

"Morning, your man was looking for you," she says slyly.

I roll my eyes. "Shut up Jozlyn and mind someone hears you saying that bullshit." I instinctively check to see if anyone heard.

"Relax, I'm joking," she laughs, "But yeah he came by your desk maybe ten minutes ago looking for you."

I glance at Lancaster's office and see him sitting at his desk. "Guess I'll go see what he wants."

"Bet you're in trouble. Maybe someone didn't suck him off good last night, I could teach you," she winks at me.

I get up from my desk and head towards Lancaster's office. "Fuck off Jozlyn," I hiss. She flips me the bird and I roll my eyes.

Lancaster is perusing some documents when I get to his office door. Each time he's done reading a page the paper would rise and place itself at the top of another stack of papers to the right of his desk. I knock three times against his door. He looks up and gives me a small smile.

"Mathieu, come on in. Guess you heard I was looking for you this morning."

I return his smile and walk into his office. He motions for me to sit and I do. Today he wore a navy suit with a cream shirt. His striped tie was kept in place by his signature dolphin shaped tie clip. I detect a subtle masculine, almost rugged but fragrant smell. I see that he shaved this morning; it must be his aftershave. I closed my eyes for a brief second just to take it in.

"So, I got this from Karl in HR this morning he says," startling me a little as he produced a folder from his desk. His voice was measured. "Take a look."

I reach to take the folder and feel as his fingers brush mine. I glance at his hand. No ring on the left hand. I'm sure I wasn't the only one in the office who wondered why a successful and attractive man like Lancaster remained unmarried. There were rumors…

"You see why this could be a problem?" Startled again, I look down at the paper in the folder he handed me. I read the content thoroughly, raise my eyebrows then nod.

"I love having you work here. You're an important member of the team," Lancaster says. I smile and nod. "But this could be nothing. Mix-ups happen in the system all the time. You'll just need to bring your passport and valid visa tomorrow and they'll sort it out quickly."

"Of course," I smile.

"You'll be fine as long as you're straight," he says. I chuckle at this. "They just started reviewing everybody's file because of the new federal sanctions."

"Yeah I get it," my throat feels chalky, "Don't think I updated my file with HR."

"That's what I assumed, you know how Karl and the rest of HR are," Lancaster says laughing a little. He licks his bottom lip for a quick moment and I squeeze my own thigh.

"Do I keep this or –?" I ask, motioning to the folder.

"Oh, I'll take that," he reaches for the folder and I hand it back to him, purposely allowing my fingers to brush against his again. I look up at him and he seems to hold my gaze for a second. He momentarily licks his bottom lip again then breaks our gaze, putting the folder into his desk drawer. I lean back in the chair as if to relax. I know I'm supposed to be terrified but I feel safe – stupidly – in Lancaster's office. As if nothing can get me here. "That was all," Lancaster says, interrupting my thoughts.

"Oh… yeah," I get up from the chair and go back to my desk. When I sit down, Jozlyn rolls over to my workstation as per usual.

"So do you still want lessons, or…?" she quips.

"You really do need to fuck off," I tell her, chuckling a little.

I do my usual evening ritual when I get home that evening. Tonight, I'm watching *Burning Thrones*. This was one of the most anticipated episodes of the season. The opposing army had marched into Glaslin and destroyed their magic reserves in the last episode. Thus, hindering the protagonists' magic and disconnecting the people from nature and their land. This new episode is exciting because the protagonists have to find a way to defeat the invaders without access to their natural magic.

I dig into my steaming ramen noodles as Thom rams his sword through Denys. I knew Denys' time was coming, a major character had to die. As Denys' men fall back, I hear a knock at the door. I reach for the remote and lower the volume on the TV.

"Who is it?" I call.

"Open up!" came the reply.

I sigh and increase the volume on the TV, leaning back into the chair. I am scared. Not that anyone would know.

Charity

The air itself was already thick. Thick with anger, frustration, and rage. Thick with hatred. The anger, frustration and rage came from both sides. The hate came from both sides as well. One side hated the symbol of oppression that stood for decades in front of the Madison County Courthouse, while the other side hated the first side for hating the symbol of oppression that they loved. The pickup truck only came from one side. The people mowed down all were on one side. Charity Smith was only on one side.

Charity threw herself to the left of the steps of the courthouse, landing in the freshly cut grass. She heard a loud snap as she landed on her right arm. She stifled a scream as the black pickup sped past her, up the steps of the courthouse, taking down dozens of people in its path.

Placards, signs, flags and human bodies flew in every direction as Charity watched, tears streaming down her face, mouth agape and an unnatural bulge on her left arm. The black pickup then proceeded to reverse down the courthouse steps, running over anything or anybody that remained in its way. Its windows were darkly tinted, old dirt stuck to the sides of the vehicle and its left taillight was out. Most noticeable – at least to Charity – was the confederate flag on the vanity license plate – which read CARL – on the truck.

As it hit the street, it sped off down the road and made a sharp left at the first intersection, leaving a fine cloud of dust hanging in the air.

Fears, Fantasies & Freedom

How thick was the air? Much thicker than how we started out. It was still thick with anger, frustration, rage and hatred, but now death, terror and weeping joined the aforementioned. Charity finally looked down at her left arm, a bone seemed to be pushing to find a way outside of her body. Pain coursed through her entire body even though it appeared that she had only injured her arm. The wailing and crying in the atmosphere filled her ears.

Only hours ago, these voices were raised in defiance and outrage against the Confederate monument that had graced the front of the courthouse in Huntsville for as long as Charity or her parents (or their parents) could remember. What had started out as a robust rally now sounded like multiple, simultaneous funerals. Charity struggled to her feet for a better view of her surroundings. She scowled as she saw the monument on the pedestal: a bearded man made of marble with a rifle in his hand. The inscription on the pedestal read:

IN MEMORY OF THE HEROES WHO FELL IN DEFENSE OF THE PRINCIPLES WHICH GAVE BEARTH TO THE CONFEDEARTE CAUSE. ERECTED BY THE DAUGHTERS OF THE CONFEDERACY.

Pinpricks of sunlight poked through the large tree above her that shaded her from the sweltering Alabama summer heat. Black tire marks stained the cream-colored pavement that led up to the stairs of the courthouse. The first two bodies lay there. One of them was a man, black slacks, red plaid shirt. A sign that read NO TRUMP, NO KKK, NO FASCIST USA lay next to him, soaking in the puddle of blood that formed around his head. The second body was that of a woman. Her neck twisted at a grotesque angle; blood ran down the side of her mouth. Two college aged men knelt by her, crying.

Charity looked around for her husband and her friends. She could not spot them on the pavement. She walked onto the pavement, eyes scanning the crowd frantically. Sirens pierced the monotony of the wailing screams that had continued relentlessly since the pickup had sped off. Police cars and ambulance vehicles pulled up to the curb as Charity pushed through the crowd with one arm, fighting to go up the courthouse stairs. The pain in her left arm throbbed repeatedly as if to the rhythm of the sirens.

"LEON!" she shouted, probably in vain. The cacophony of weeping, shouting, shuffling and sirens was hard to break through.

"LYRA! CALVIN!" she tried again. As she got close to the top of the stairs, she heard her name.

Fears, Fantasies & Freedom

"CHARITY! CHARITY!" Charity peeked over the shoulder of a man in front of her. "Leon!" she cried, pushing past the man and running into her husband's outstretched arms. As he embraced her, Charity felt something like hope wash over her. Her arm was broken and the protest may have gone to shit but she still had her Leon and no amount of magic would be enough to compare to how she felt in this moment. She sobbed into her husband's T-shirt, taking in his scent, appreciating his warmth.

"Are you okay?" he asked.

She broke his embrace and looked up at him. His brown eyes were surrounded with red; he'd been crying.

"My arm's broken," she replied, "I'll be fine though, where are the others?"

Leon took a while to answer. His eyes slowly welled up with tears as he motioned behind him with his head.

Charity looked behind her husband and spotted her friends Calvin and Reina stooping on the ground, shaking. No, sobbing. Both. Charity could not see what they were surrounding, but she did spot a red Converse poking out next to Reina's leg.

"Where's Lyra?" Charity asked, looking up at her husband.

"Charity, I –" he began.

"Leon, where is Lyra?" Charity questioned again, her voice rising.

"It's so bad babe," he sobbed, "It's so bad…"

Charity could hardly breathe as she walked over to where Calvin and Reina stooped on the floor. All of a sudden, she seemed to notice blue ripples in the air, as if the air was collapsing on itself. It's hard to explain. The ripples seemed to be some disruption of the reality. As Charity reached where Calvin and Reina squatted, she could clearly see Reina lying on the ground, eyes closed, blood leaking through a gash on her forehead. Her world really was collapsing on itself.

"Is she?" she started.

Reina, Lyra's wife, would not answer, her hair was disheveled and face tear-stained. Calvin nodded. Charity fell.

"Nooooo!" she screamed. She wrapped her one good arm around Lyra's body and wept. She placed her hand on Lyra's chest and summoned her magic, shooting it straight into her chest, a shower of sparks quickly appearing then disappearing.

"Charity, stop." Calvin sobbed, "We already tried."

Charity summoned some more magic and tried again. Lyra did not respond. Charity shot another dose of magic into Lyra's chest; in vain. A soft voice behind her said, "Stop."

Fears, Fantasies & Freedom

She dropped her hand and hung her head. She didn't know how many cantas of magic she probably just spent. She didn't care. She closed her eyes and let the sounds of the sirens and the wailings wash over her.

Michael/Itza Feary

"Good evening, everybody, welcome to the show!"

You hear the audience roar with cheers and applause after Ma Mary Glanz opens the Friday night show. You're a little nervous. It's only your third show.

"The rules of engagement are really quite simple," Ma Mary continues after the applause quiets down, "If you happen to be sitting in the front row, stay of ya fuckin' phone! It's really quite simple."

"The queens are here to entertain you and these bitches *lahve* attention so give it to them. Second of all, don't touch the performers. It takes a lotta money to look this cheap honey, so if you fuck up a bitch wig, you gon' pay for it!"

You smile as you adjust your own wig. You reach for the wig glue on the counter next to the hairspray and apply a smidge under the lace of the wig next to your right ear. You check the mirror to make sure the wig looks good. You're satisfied.

Fears, Fantasies & Freedom

You quickly glance behind you to check out the other gals in the dressing room. Lykra Chorts' perfect beat reflects back at you from her mirror. Her makeup brush hovers gracefully, lightly retouching her blush. Lykra nonchalantly flicks her fingers and a lipstick floats up from her counter, uncaps itself and applies a fresh coat to her lips. Next to her, Agave Dickila is bent forward in her chair, apparently attaching rhinestones to her stockings.

"And the last rule is: tip these MEN!" exclaims Ma Mary as the crowd goes wild yet again. "The illusion you see on this stage tonight is due to the fabulous work by our extraordinary performers. I know them bitches in the back will tell you they woke up like this, but trust me, I've seen Ms. Agave at 3AM on a Tuesday night, or is that Wednesday morning? Either way, the bitch is ugly."

The crowd shrieks with laughter and whistles. You distinctly hear someone shout 'SHADE!' and another fit of laughter erupts from the audience.

"I got my nuts in my guts and my dick pulled back on my taint. So, this is called commitment, bitch! Tip a hoe!" You hear Ma Mary say. "Thank you dahling, she got on a Burberry sweater so she ain't poor!"

Fears, Fantasies & Freedom

You delicately retrace the eyeliner already blackening your lash line just for good measure. You smile a little. Your make-up looks better than it did last week at your first shows. You marvel at how much your blending has improved since starting to experiment with makeup, you can hardly see where the lace on the wig begins. Your painted-on eyebrows are like twin hills looming over the beautiful landscape that is you face. Your real eyebrows are buried under a thick coating of Elmer's glue stick, foundation, powder and the most delicate rose-colored hue extending onto your eyelids and wrapping around the corners of your eye. You blink a couple times as you get used to the amber contacts in your eyes. You laugh a little as you hear the queens behind you playfully insulting each other. Your nose looks smaller and thinner and you smile as you remember how long it took you to master a realistic looking nose contour. Your lips are painted a color similar to your eye makeup. Instinctively, you reach for the lipstick on the counter and apply a little more to your lips. Pink and turquoise jewels drip from your ears, slightly brushing your collarbone when you move your head. On the counter is a fresh pack of lashes. You pick it up with the corresponding glue next to it and attach the long 13 mm, curled lashes on your eyelids. Consulting the mirror, you tease your rosé-tinted hair cascading around your shoulders and flowing down your back. You remove a hairbrush from

Fears, Fantasies & Freedom

the counter and slowly run it through your hair.

"You look beautiful, newbie," a voice says behind you.

You turn around and there stands Lady Die, smiling down at you.

"Thank you," you say shyly. "You of course, look phenomenal as usual."

"Well thank you darling, I just pulled this ol' thing together," Die says, giving a little twirl in her black and silver bodysuit. She saunters over to the empty chair in the makeup area next to you. "I hear your first show was last weekend, how was it?"

"Pretty great… I think," you say.

"You think?"

"Well, I mean, it wasn't anything like what you do," you offer sheepishly.

"Honey, not everyone does what I do," Die smiles, "Not everyone *can* do what I do. Drag is an art form, you don't need to copy anyone, it's whatever you make it."

"Ain't nobody wanna do what you do bitch!" shouts Lykra, cackling from across the room.

Lady Die stands and flips off Lykra, "You wish you could do this honey. I know you're jealous but I'm jealous too, I hear they're casting the next season of *Finding Bigfoot* and the rumor mill is churning that you're a frontrunner to be cast. It's a popular show, I hope they do eventually *find* you." She punctuates this by blowing a kiss at Lykra while Agave guffaws over at her mirror. You try to stifle a laugh but you end up bursting out screaming with mirth.

"Now That's What You Call Reading Vol. 7 now available in stores or wherever this shady bitch Lady Die sells them," Agave says, still laughing.

The moment of lighthearted ribbing comes to an end as you all hear Ma Mary Glanz announce that Lykra Chorts would be next on the stage.

"That's my cue gals, wish me luck," she says blowing a kiss at the room. The hem of her peach silky wrap dress is the last you see of her as she disappears around the corner to get on stage. Immediately, from around the same corner, a tall, busty person walks into the room, with a microphone in hand. She is wearing a royal blue, form-fitting dress that stops just above her knees and a short, black wig. She looks almost exactly like Patti Labelle.

Fears, Fantasies & Freedom

"It's a great crowd tonight," Ma Mary Glanz says as she walks in and throws herself in the chair next to you. She might look like Patti but her voice confirms that she could never sing like Patti. "How are you, Michael? Nervous?"

"A little," you say, "But I'm excited."

"Good, just give it your all. A hen party is here tonight so give those drunk bitches their entire life and get your life too, honey."

Ma Mary spins in her chair and addresses the entire room, "Everybody good? Pumped? Excited?"

"Excited to get these *cantas* mama!" Agave says, sipping on a cocktail.

"I'm so glad to be back though, I missed you guys," Lady Die declares.

"The superstar is back to mingle with the peasants," Ma Mary laughs, "But seriously bitch you gotta fill us all in on all your world travels and nationwide tours and all that."

You are mesmerized by Lady Die. She had become an actual celebrity in the last six months after appearing on a popular drag queen competition TV show and placing in the Top 3. Her confidence and poise are off the charts and it was obvious that she was raking in loads of *cantas*. Her wig seems to glisten as she recounts tales of her adventures abroad.

Fears, Fantasies & Freedom

She was no longer just a local bar queen; she is an international star and it is obvious. The crowds tonight did not come for Lykra or Agave or yourself; they came for Lady Die. Their local queen had become a legitimate star and everyone wanted a piece of her. You remember about a year ago when you were sitting on the curb just outside the club with Lady Die out of drag waiting for an Uber. Back then he just seemed like any other regular person, today she exudes regality.

You hear Lykra's number coming to an end on the stage. Ma Mary quiets the dressing room, points her head toward you and winks. You immediately stand up and start adjusting your dress, making sure the breastplate sits comfortably under the fabric. As you do minor touch-ups to your makeup in the mirror, Ma Mary raises the microphone to her lips. You hear the music from the stage end and the applause slowly dies down.

"Out next is the newest girl in our family, y'all might know her from the closest bathroom stall but I know her as my drag daughter. It's not a bird, it's not a plane: Itza Feary! Put your hands together!" Ma Mary screams into the microphone with as much gusto as if the audience were sitting here in the dressing room with her.

Lykra walks in as soon as Ma Mary is finished speaking.

Fears, Fantasies & Freedom

"It really is a great crowd tonight, I got so much magic I could be Lady Die's sugar daddy!" The dressing room bursts into laughter as you head out onto the stage.

The club is dark as you step on the stage. There is almost a hush over the crowd. Your head is bowed and you stand with a power pose, waiting for the music to start. You've practiced this lip-sync routine every day this week and you're ready to show the audience what you're made of. A spotlight comes on pointed directly at you. The music starts and immediately whatever nervousness you felt dissipates. It's a Britney mashup, with all her greatest hits. You mouth the words precisely, punctuating each beat with a hair flip, some hand choreography and some high energy strutting.

The crowd is going wild. The euphoria is almost overwhelming. And then you feel it: the first hit of magic. You look over at the guy who shot it and blow him a kiss while hitting every mark in your choreography. Immediately, the rooms light up with blue sparks as the patrons shoot magic tips after magic tips. The more magic they tip, the more high-energy your performance becomes.

The audience is singing and dancing along with you. You know that the big zenith of the song is coming and you prepare yourself for the move you've been practicing since the day you decided you would become a drag queen. Here it comes. You leap into the air, extend your right leg and curl your left leg for cushion. You fall to the floor, arms wide; a perfect landing. A perfect dip.

The audience is out of it. You hear screams of "YAAAAAASSSSSS!" as you are showered with double doses of magic. You reckon you might make way more tips tonight than what the club actually pays you for a booking fee. As you jump to your feet, you prepare for the transition to the last song in the mashup, and it was a big one. As the beat drops, you pull off your rosé-colored wig to reveal a royal blue, pixie-cut wig underneath. Then you pull against the inconspicuous Velcro at the back of your dress to expose a chic blue and black leotard perfect for the insane choreography in the final song.

At this point the onlookers seem to become rabid as they shoot copious amounts of magic at you; glee and excitement painting their faces. You hit the final move as the music stops, breathing heavily as the applause and acclaim wash over you. 'This is *it*,' you think. This is the reason why you chose this profession.

Fears, Fantasies & Freedom

Nothing compares to the adulation one gets from screaming fans (and *paying* fans). The lights go down as you head off the stage. You hear Ma Mary Glanz announce Agave as the next performer as you enter the dressing room.

"Bitch you killed it!" Agave whispers as she walks past you.

Ma Mary Glanz rushes to give you a hug, "That was amazing Michael, we all were watching from the side." The other queens in the room nod and smile enthusiastically

"You got something kid, that was impressive," Lady Die says from her station as Ma Mary releases you. You walk over to your mirror and sit down, still a little out of breath.

"Thank you, guys, it means a lot. I worked really hard on this one."

"And you've got the *cantas* to prove it bitch," Lykra remarks, "I saw you getting all that magic out there."

"A couple more performances like that and I think they just might raise your booking fee," Ma Mary notes, looking intently at you.

Lady Die stands up and walks over to you. She stands behind you, looking in the mirror for a few seconds. Then she slowly bends until her face is next to yours.

"I hear they're looking for a new superstar, that could be you," she whispers and winks as you hear the music for Agave's number begin on stage.

"You think it was that good Ryan?" You ask Ma Mary Glanz from the bathroom.

"I could say, that for a newbie you were really good," Ryan shouts back from the living room, "But I'm saying that performance was amazing, for *any* drag queen. Point. Blank. And the period."

You massage the oil cleanser into your face as you step out into the living room, where Ryan is lounging on the couch watching TV.

"Yo, I made so much magic tonight I can afford to not only buy new wigs but use magic for day-to-day stuff," you remark, as the makeup on your face gently melts away.

"Don't go spending it all now Michael," Ryan tuts, "I remember when I just started being Ma Mary Glanz twelve years ago and I was rich all weekend and by Wednesday I was broke again."

You step back into the bathroom and grab a wet cloth to wipe off the oil cleanser and makeup on your face. "I mean I'm not gonna start levitating around the place or shoot fireballs like a maniac," you say. You pick up a bottle off the bathroom counter and squirt a big glob of facial cleanser into your palm. You rub it together with your hands then apply the lather to your face. You take your time rubbing the foam into your cheeks, around your nose and eyes.

"You think I could get as big as Die?" you enquire, poking your head out of the bathroom.

Fears, Fantasies & Freedom

"You young queens," Ryan sighs, turning to look at you, "Honey you only started performing last week. Focus on the shit you got going on now. The rest will come when it should."

You nod as Ryan turns back to the TV. You duck back into the bathroom and turn on the faucet. The cool water makes your face tingle as it reacts with the mint in the facial cleaner. You reach for a towel as you look at your fresh face in the mirror. Your ears perk up as the volume on the TV in the living room increases. It's the news.

"Michael, you hearing this shit?" Ryan calls.

You open a packet on the bathroom counter and pull out a lemon-scented exfoliating pad. You rub this into your face as you step into the living room once more.

"No, what's that?" you ask, looking at the TV.

"You remember about that guy running that trafficking shit?" Ryan asks.

"Yeah," I say as the picture of the man and his wife appear on the screen.

"Apparently, the wife was in on it too. Sick bitch was just on TV last week defending him bout 'suspects are innocent until proven otherwise."

"I hope they throw away the fucking key after they lock them both up," you say, stepping back into the bathroom.

"All those black girls," Ryan says, "Years and not a soul could find them. I'm just glad they caught these sick fucks. Some people will do the worst shit to hurt our community."

You sigh as you think about the campaign to find the missing black girls starting almost three years ago.

You pour some toner on a cotton pad and start dabbing away at your face with it.

"Ryan?"

"Sup?" he calls back.

"I just wanna say thanks for everything," you say. "A place to live, guidance with drag, getting me the gig, just taking me under your wing on a whole."

"Michael, you're my friend, I wasn't gonna see you broke and down on your luck and not try to help you." Ryan replies. He gets up from the couch and walks over to the bathroom door; stopping to lean on the door post. "I started drag at 17, back then, we never had the resources y'all queens have today. There were no award-winning TV shows, no social media, no multi-million magic-making tours. But what we did have was a family. I ain't know what I would've done without my drag mama back then."

You smile at Ryan while putting a green tea-infused mask on your face.

"Bitch, I can't take you seriously with that shit on your face," Ryan laughs, walking back over to the couch.

"You gotta get into this face mask life girl, it does wonders for your skin," you offer.

"You young queens," Ryan chuckles. You can almost imagine her rolling her eyes as she says this.

It's Saturday night. You're standing at the corner of the stage with Agave, Ma Mary, Lykra. Lady Die is performing and as per usual, it is breathtaking. She is doing a burlesque number where she performs literal circus moves on a ring suspended from the ceiling. Articles of clothing litter the stage from what Die had already removed from her body.

She is still wearing a large peacock feather headpiece and a black feather boa around her shoulders. The crowd is dousing her in magic (not like she needs it; her booking fee is 8 times what the rest of the queens make) while she does a handstand spread-eagle on the ring *while* lip-syncing to Janet Jackson. The club promoters must be ecstatic. The crowds last night and tonight were overwhelming and drinks are flying off the bar. Lady Die was the perfect show closer and the promoters made sure to exploit the opportunity as best they could by charging a meet and greet fee to meet Die along with the standard cover to get into the club. It's amazing what 4 months on a TV show can do to one's celebrity.

You watch as Lady Die does a backflip off the ring and just before she is supposed to land on the floor, she soars into the air, shooting golden sparkles from the tips of her fingers, showering the crowd. In response, the crowd shoots blue currency sparks at her. You wonder how rich some of these people are. Lady Die ends her performance with nothing but crystal-encrusted pasties on her boy-nipples and a matching pair of tiny panties. As the crowd erupts, you and the other queens go back to the dressing room. Everyone does a little touch up to their makeup as Lady Die enters the room. Ma Mary Glanz goes out on the stage for the curtain call.

"She's the belle of the ballad but also the baddest bitch in this bar, put your hand together for Lykra Chorts!" Ma Mary Glanz shouts. Lykra heads out onto the stage.

"You all love her, and I can't stand the bitch. It's a bird? No. It's a plane? No. Itza Feary!" At this cue, you run out onto the stage. The audience is standing and applauding. You blow them kisses then bow, before going to the back of the stage to stand next to Lykra.

"She's a Mexican alcoholic who you can always call for a good time. Welcome Agave Dickila! Clap for this hooker!"

Agave runs on to the stage, waving and blowing kisses at the audience. She curtsies then comes to the back of the stage with you and Lykra.

"She's the demure debutante, the A-list acrobatic, the serene celebrity, the show-stopping superstar and an all-round whore! Put your hands together for Lady Die!"

Die receives the loudest applause. She skips onto the stage, waving to the crowd. She forms her right hand to look like a phone, then places it at her ear and mouths 'Call me' then winks. Two blue sparks come from somewhere in the audience and Die grins as she accepts them. She bows and walks over to Ma Mary Glanz who hands her the microphone.

"I want all of you to put your hands together for the hardest working queen in this city! She's the bitch who keeps this shit running and your host for tonight: Ma Mary Glanz!" shouts Lady Die.

Ma Mary beams as she does a little curtsy. You, Agave and Lykra walk to the center of the stage where Ma Mary and Lady Die stand and you all hold hands in a line. You all bow four times amidst applause. It's a wrap.

There's a little bit of a chill in the wind tonight. The streets are pretty scanty as it usually is at this time of the night. You're walking with Carl; he was at the show earlier tonight. He says he's your biggest fan and waited at the door backstage to get a chance to speak with you.

"I mean; how much do you think we make?" you ask him.

"Quite a lot it seems, enough to make you look as pretty as you do now," he flirts.

"Not as much as you would think," you say. You're about three blocks from Ryan's apartment. Ryan had said he was sleeping at his partner's home tonight, so it would just be you.

"Don't lie bae," Carl says, sidling closer to you. He has long greasy, black hair and a hooked nose. His eyes are dark and he has a square jaw. At certain angles and in a certain light, he could be described as handsome to someone. His dark clothes blend in with the night. His trench coat billows slightly in the gentle breeze. You smell tequila on his breath.

"It's not nice to call someone you just met a liar," you say, looking at him.

"It's not nice to lie," he says. You think you detect a slight edge to his voice.

"Thanks for walking with me," you say, "I live a couple blocks from here. I can take it from here."

"You don't want me?" he enquires, sounding almost offended.

"I've been in make-up, heels and a dress all night. I'm a man in a wig and my junk is tucked away under miles of tape and pantyhose. It's 4 AM and I'm tired, I just want to sleep," you explain, crossing the street. He follows next to you. You're only a block away from home now. You hear a dog howling somewhere on the block.

"I want some," Carl says, grabbing your arm.

"Let go of me," you say, shrugging him off, "I think you probably had too much to drink." You spot the apartment a few yards away. You shiver a little as you feel a draft blow through the alley that you're walking past.

"I said I want some now!" Carl growls and he pushes you in the alley. He wraps his hand around your throat and holds you against the wall.

"Get the fuck off me!" you shout.
He slaps you across the face and uses his other hand to cover your mouth. His face is right up against yours. His hot tequila breath hits you as the hair in your nostrils bristle. You can hardly breathe. You realize blue ripples in the air, seemingly closing in on you. The ripples appear to distort space. You're probably about to pass out.

"I saw how much magic they shoved at you tonight bitch, lemme get some."

Fears, Fantasies & Freedom

You struggle against his grip and he releases your throat. He shoves his hand into his trench coat and pulls out a small silver knife. He places the blade at your throat as a low growl escapes his lips. "Still think I'm playing?"

You're pissed at the fact that you're about to lose a good chunk of the magic you earned tonight. You summon it and send a telekinetic wave at Carl, releasing yourself from his grip and slamming him into the opposite wall. He slumps to the ground as the knife flies out of his hand, into the darkness of the alley.

"I told you to get off me!" you snarl, looking down at him.

"Telekinesis on a person?" Carl says, struggling to his feet, "You *really* do make a lot."

You turn to run but are interrupted by a force tugging at your foot. You lose your balance and fall face down in the alley. He was using magic as well. You struggle against the force, but he pulls you toward him and locks your arms and legs together. He is standing upright now, and with a flick of his head, you are against the wall again; unable to move. He flicks his head again and the knife floats out of the darkness and rests at your throat. You stupidly think about the fact that they're going to find you dead with a face full of makeup, no wig, a dirty dress and some beat-up sneakers. A mess, really.

Fears, Fantasies & Freedom

"Pass over the magic or you're done," he says. You do nothing. The knife flies from your throat and immediately digs itself into your side. You let out a scream as the pain rips you apart. You think about the fact that you would rather be poor than dead. Tears are running down your face.

"If you want it, take it!" you sob. You summon the magic. You watch as a fireball forms in front of you and slams Carl in the chest. A look of horror passes over his face as he is once again slammed into the opposite wall. His telekinetic grip loosens and you wince at the smell of burning fabric, flesh and hair. You touch your side, where the knife is lodged. It's drenched in blood. You take a few steps then collapse. You ruined a good dress.

Fears, Fantasies & Freedom

Carlton

The three prisoners looked peaceful as they slept. Straps kept them secured to the tables. It was time for their execution. Carlton was used to having prisoners, and killing them. If you did wrong, then you deserve the full extent of the law. He walked over to the first table and picked up a file on the desk next to it. MATHIEU MARTIN was the name at the top of the file. Carlton shook his head, 'Goddamn illegals,' he thought. This one had come from the Bahamas and was staying in the country illegally for some time. He was making a solid amount of magic, sending some back for his family in the Bahamas. There are no second chances when you lie to the government. Carlton pushed his greasy hair from in front of his eyes as he walked to the next table.

He picked up the file next to the woman. Her name was CHARITY SMITH; some black activist. She was accused of inciting violence in Alabama by helping to organize a demonstration because of a statue. Lots of good men and women suffered because this bitch couldn't sit down and not upset the establishment. Apparently, her friend got killed by the pickup driver than ran over the crowd. She should've gotten hit too, maybe then she'd have learnt a lesson.

Fears, Fantasies & Freedom

Carlton, looked over at the next one. He didn't need an introduction and Carlton didn't need to read his file. That was Michael Green: The Flame Killer. He was a drag queen that went by the name Itza Feary. He claimed that he was attacked by his victim but nobody really believed him. Who was walking around blasting people with fireballs in this day and age? It was a huge media story. When investigations revealed that he used extensive telekinesis on the victim, it was fairly obvious that this motherfucker was just a cold-blooded killer.

Carlton walked over to the monitors on the wall opposite the tables. The sterile room had a slight chill. He thought it was time to wake them up. He pressed a few buttons on the screen and turned around to face the prisoners. Their eyes fluttered open. Mathieu tore off his straps and sat up, looking straight at Carlton. Fear crawled up Carlton's spine. He wasn't in control. Mathieu easily did away the straps on his legs and rolled off the table. He walked over to Charity and tore off her straps as well. Both of them walked to Michael's table and removed his straps. All three stared at Carlton.

"You like keeping prisoners, Carlton?" Michael asked. A fireball formed in front of him and flew at Carlton's head. Carlton ducked and fled for the door. All three prisoners followed after him. He opened the door and ran down the proceeding hallway. The lights in the hallway kept flickering as Carlton ran.

"You like keeping prisoners, Carlton?" Charity shouted behind him.

Carlton kept running, fear gripping his insides. There were no doors in the hallway and he kept looking to see when the hallway would end. He kept running. The three prisoners were gaining on him. They were all shouting in unison, "You like keeping prisoners Carlton?" The hallway seemed endless. Carlton looked behind him, they were gaining on him. As he ran, he noticed blue ripples closing in on him in the hallway. It's like his entire reality was falling apart. He kept running. The blue ripples continue to close in. He was breathing hard. The prisoners were right behind him now. The blue ripples were now blue waves, tearing at the fabric of space. Then, nothing.

"How was that simulation, Dr. Smith?" Dr. Mathieu Martin asks.

"I think I'll leave him in this one for a while. The endless hallway was a good idea," Dr. Charity Smith replies.

Fears, Fantasies & Freedom

"He liked keeping children as prisoners, the sick fuck," the other doctor in the room said.

"Well, Michael," Dr. Martin responds, "He's got fifty years of this. The whole magic alternate dimension was a great idea."

"I mean, it's brilliant. A world with magic but everything is still shitty." Michael says.

"Turn on the simulation again Charity, we should leave him running in that hallway for the weekend," Mathieu suggests.

"Sounds good. When we return, we can start the simulations all over again. Make him think he has control, until he realizes that he doesn't" she laughs.

The other doctors laugh along with her as Carlton Tierney groans strapped to his table while images of illegal immigrants, confederate statues, drag queens, magic, fireballs and child trafficking rings haunt him.

Acknowledgements

This project would have been impossible to complete without the help and support of a number of wonderful individuals. I will start out by thanking my best friend Odaine and my Tongue Pop group: Bradley, Claudio, Francois Kwame, Riki and Omar for pushing me and encouraging me along this journey.

Next, I'd like to thank my family members who listen to me talk on and on about this project for years as I was compiling and writing. So huge thanks to my mother, my father, my aunties Karen, Dena & Jennifer and my fabulous cousins, Derrick, Kareena and Ashley.

Much gratitude to the Goddess of DC, Rayceen Pendarvis who took me under her wing and gave me a space and a platform to spread my own wings. Special thanks to Niqui and Zar from Team Rayceen Productions for always being there to support and promote my endeavors.

This project is what it is in huge part to the contributions of Robert Garcia, Barry Feinstein, Olivia Miles and Earl Melvin. Huge thanks to the cast and crew of the *Leave the Door Open* stage play. You all helped my dream come true.

Thank you to Marlon James for inspiring me.

Thank you to my English professors at Howard University and my favorite English teacher from Munro College, Marjorie Simpson.

Thank you to the countless other friends, family members and individuals who provided any modicum of support, advice and well-wishes along this journey.

Thank you to Maurice Williams for being my rock and putting up with the delays, long nights and emotional distance we endured during this process. Love is love.

Like Lady Gaga said: there could be a hundred people in a room and ninety-nine don't believe in you but all you need is just one to believe, and it could change your life. I'm grateful, honored and humbled to say there were far more than only one person in the room who believed in me.

-Krylios

Fears, Fantasies & Freedom

Made in the USA
Middletown, DE
19 May 2023